Gold Mine in Wales
Vandalized

Gwen Bohlen

Previous Books by Gwen Bohlen:
Penfields & Esteps, A Tale of Two Colonial Families & Their Part
in the Settling of the West
Welsh Knights' Relic, A Detective Owain Wallon Mystery

ISBN: 1456583433
ISBN-13: 9781456583439
LCCN: 2011901570

Table of Contents

LIST OF CHARACTERS IN
Gold Mine in Wales Vandalized

Chief Inspector Owain Wallon

Tom Lewis and Gwyneth Lydley Lewis and her brother Guy Lydley

Hywel Gorwyn and Catherine Gorwyn, Owain Wallon's aunt and uncle

Inspector Louis Duvrey, and team Ted Sutter, Bill Denton, John Older, Burt Dagart

Detective Sergeant Clyde McDowell of Scotland Yard Special Branch

Superintendent Edwin Cadwell and Detective Floyd Jones from the district police station in North Wales

Glyn Anderson, professor of geology

Francesca and James Montgomery and their older brother, Harold

Dirk Otis Shedweld

Joanna Whitecoft and her father Lord Peter Whitecoft and brothers, Albert and George

Professor Glyn Anderson of geology and his team of investigators Edward Grant, professor anthropology and Brian Holmes, professor of archeology

Inspector Jed Hawkins from Sydney Australia

PRELUDE TO
Gold Mine in Wales Vandalized

In this book, which is the second in the series, *Welsh Knights' Relic* being the first, Inspector Owain Wallon has been promoted to chief inspector of the Special Branch of Scotland Yard. His predecessor, Chief Inspector Hadley has retired. With his new responsibilities Owain misses the aid of his best friend, Inspector Tom Lewis. However, early in the story Owain is assisted by the very able Sergeant Clyde McDowell in the investigation of the infamous drug cartel cases. Tom Lewis has married Gwyneth Lydley and together they manage a very fine seaside resort hotel on the coast of North Wales called The Ormes Victoria. Many of the other characters from the previous book appear in this one. Aunt Catherine and Uncle Hywel of Gorwyn Hall are involved. There are new characters as well. Also, Lord Peter Whitecoft and his lovely, vivacious daughter, Lady Joanna, become victims of a scheming business operator as well as in gold mine criminal activities. The story winds its way through the beautiful hiking areas of Snowdonia in Wales, and to England and Australia. Murder and suicide occur to entrap Joanna and challenge Chief Inspector Owain Wallon to establish her innocent involvement in the crimes. Keeping guard are the two guardian spirits, the Welsh Templar knights Owain Pentwyn and Guy Pentwyn Lydley.

Lost Cave in Snowdonia

In the dramatic, rugged rocky terrain of the northern region of Wales, the rain poured down. A young couple caught in an unexpected storm sought shelter. They had lost their way back to the main hiking trail.

"Gwyneth, we must find cover. We're soaking wet, and the rain shows no sign of stopping," called out Tom.

With her long blond hair clinging to the side of her face under the hood of her hiking jacket, Gwyneth shouted in Tom's direction, "Look up to your left. I think I can see a rock ledge overhang of some kind above us which could give us shelter until the rain stops."

Tom looked in the direction she was pointing. "Are you ready for a climb? The ground is saturated and slippery. I'm going up first," said Tom as he brought out his climbing rope and started in the direction of the rock ledge outcropping above them. "You can follow me, or wait here." Tom was an experienced climber, and had been an inspector with Scotland Yard's Special Branch before they were married.

"I'm coming with you," Gwyneth said in Tom's ear. She secured their backpacks to the end of her rope and pulled the packs up behind her as she followed Tom up the slope towards the ledge. Just as they approached the steepest part, she roped her backpack to a tree using a slip knot. Then she started to climb using Tom's secured line. Tom had reached the ledge; now he pulled Gwyneth up the rest of the way. The rock face of the steepest part was very slippery and taking all her strength to reach him. As they searched the damp, cold ledge, they looked for a dry spot; Tom pointed to a dark dry area further back from the edge of the ledge.

"There. . . I think I can see an area where we can crawl under the overhanging rock."

Gwyneth yanked the slip knot on the end of her rope, and Tom helped her pull up the backpack, which contained a thermos of coffee and bottled water, as well as energy bars. They carefully made their way towards the dry part in the back under the ledge. Soon they located a flat spot with room for them to crouch down for cover.

"This won't do for very long. Maybe we should investigate, and see if there is a dryer space further back. Leave the backpack here, and let's keep crawling further under the ledge," said Tom. Gwyneth nodded in agreement.

Tom pulled out his torch and continued crawling farther back into the cramped dark space. He felt cold air ahead of him. Hoping that they might find an opening into a cave, Tom squeezed forward into the tight overhang area. Gwyneth, who was crawling directly behind him, heard Tom let out a string of expletives.

"Tom, what's that all about?" She laughed.

"Rats!" said Tom.

"Live rats?"

"Yes, very much alive," called back Tom.

"Ugh! What can we do? Fire and smoke should chase off the rats. I know how we can make a small fire to chase them away." She crawled back to where they had left her backpack. Grabbing a note pad and dry matches from the pack, she made her way over to Tom.

"Here, take the paper from my note pad and the matches," said Gwyneth. Tom put his hand behind him and took the pad and matches from her. He made a small wad of paper, and then told Gwyneth to back up while he lit the wad of paper. Just as he thought, there was a draft ahead of them. Smelling the smoke, the rats took off.

"You go back again to the ledge, and wait for me there, while I investigate the opening ahead. See if you can find something else that is not too wet which we can burn. I don't know how long the paper from your notebook will last," said Tom.

Gwyneth crawled back to the ledge and sat reprimanding herself for getting them lost. Aunt Catherine had drawn a good map for her and Tom to follow. However, she had felt adventurous and wanted to try this side trail that was not on the map. Now, the nice day had changed, and the rain had soaked them through. There was no way to contact Gorwyn Hall, where they were staying for the weekend. She grumbled to herself while she quickly poured a warm cup of coffee from her thermos for Tom. At that moment, she heard Tom crawling back in her direction.

"Gwyneth, we can't go up there into the cave," Tom said grimly.

"Why not?" Gwyneth questioned him. "Is it the rats?"

"No, worse than that," stated Tom. "Right now the only thing that we can do is stay here, and as soon as the rain lets up, we must lower ourselves down and find our way back to the main trail. We need to reach Owain." Owain Wallon was Tom's best friend and a chief inspector at Scotland Yard.

"What can be in the cave that is so terrible?" Gwyneth asked.

"Human remains—skeletons, bodies," explained Tom.

"Bodies?"

Back at Gorwyn Hall, Catherine looked worried as she gazed out of the window. She could see that the rain storm had started to let up after a very strong downpour. The poor young couple, Tom and Gwyneth, must be soaked and maybe lost. If they had followed her map to the waterfalls and then turned around, they should be back by now. She walked over to the library where Hywel, her brother, and their nephew, Owain, were chatting away. Owain, who was recently promoted to chief inspector at Scotland Yard's special investigation branch, enjoyed the opportunity to brush up on his Welsh conversation skills with his uncle, who encouraged speaking in the ancient language of the Welsh people. Owain was staying with them for the weekend.

Catherine moved a grey strand of hair from her face, burst into the library, and exclaimed, "I drew for Tom and Gwyneth a map of that old area back in the hills where I used to like to take walks when I was younger. I thought this sunny day would be perfect for them to hike along the old stream up there in the rocky hills and over to the waterfall. But now, this heavy rain storm has started and I'm worried about them. They should have returned by this time, wet but safe."

"Now, Catherine, calm yourself, and tell us exactly where it is that you sent Tom and Gwyneth for a hike," asked Hywel. He was very fond of his sister, but she loved to worry about people.

Owain spoke up. "Alright, Aunt Catherine, draw a map to show us where you sent them for their hike. I will take a couple of the young men from your shepherding staff and we will go find them. We will find them. Don't worry."

Catherine went to the desk to draw the map again. She put her pencil down and handed the map drawing over to Owain. He glanced at it, then handed it over to Uncle Hywel, who had lived in this part of Wales all his life.

Hywel took one look at the map and grumbled, "This trail that you sent them out to hike in, Catherine, has been closed for years by the Environmental Protection Agency of Great Britain. No one is supposed to enter this area. There are serious fines for anyone caught wandering in there."

"Well, I didn't know that. . . . Pretty soon there won't be any place we can go at all," said Catherine. She was obviously exasperated about having her favorite hiking trail closed.

"There are other reasons for this area to be off limits. Don't you remember your history, woman?" Hywel was growing impatient with her. "Celtic gold mines that had been used during Roman times were in this region. People go crazy about searching for gold. The mine was boarded up many years ago. They prohibited people from entering because of the danger of cave-ins," explained Hywel.

The brother and sister, both over sixty, tended to get irritated with each other from time to time. They had grown up together at the family's ancient home, Gorwyn Hall. Their ancestors were Welsh Templar Knights who had fought in the Holy Land before the downfall of Jerusalem. Today the estate harbored one of the finest sheep herds in all of Wales.

Their nephew Owain got to his feet and was heading towards the coat rack to put on rain gear. He was a tall, handsome man in his early thirties. "Would you send for a couple of your sheep herds-men? We must go out and find them. I will need some rope, also a first aid kit," said Owain.

Everyone rushed around and helped collect the gear that Owain requested. Outside, a Land Rover arrived with one of Catherine's supervisors and his two sons. Owain climbed in with Catherine's map, and they took off for the prohibited area.

Gorwyn Hall, where Hywel and Catherine had lived since childhood, was the ancestral home of the Gorwyn family, who were descendents of the Gruffydds in old Welsh history. The sturdy old stone farm house, built centuries earlier, had been enlarged many times, and a second floor added. After years of a successful business in sheep breeding and shearing, during Victorian times the Gorwyn family turned their old farm house into an impressive stone manor. An attractive entry at the center of Gorwyn Hall was added, along with the beautiful curved oak stairway in the center of the entrance hall.

The hills surrounding the manor and outbuildings were perfect grazing land for the family's famous breed of sheep. The wool from these sheep was of a very high quality, and prize-winning weavers sought it out. To have a scarf or blanket made from the wool of the Gorwyn sheep farm was greatly prized—and expensive. The Gorwyn crest was always featured on the label. Aunt Catherine managed the business end, and Uncle Hywel, after graduation from Oxford, had established his own law firm in town. Recently, he had retired and turned the firm over to his son-in-law, Arthur Howard and Ann, Uncle Hywel's only child. They lived in one of the spacious cottages in town. Elizabeth Gorwyn Wallon, the eldest sister of Hywel and Catherine, was chief inspector Owain's mother. She had been killed, along with her husband, in a high-speed sports car accident many years ago. The accident brought terrible grief to her remaining brother and sister. Owain's father's name, Wallon, was never mentioned again by the family at Gorwyn Hall. Thus, the identity of Edwin Wallon was unknown to Owain; and he was to seek after the information later on.

As the Land Rover splashed through the muddy back roads, Owain handed the map to Ed Gynmar, the supervisor of the sheep flocks. He took one look at the location shown on the map and said, "No one is allowed into that restricted area. We can be fined if we go there." He grumbled.

"Don't worry Ed, I am a chief inspector with Scotland Yard, and besides we are on a rescue mission."

Driving the narrow back roads, they soon reached the spot on the map where the trail began. Owain looked for signs that announced a warning to "Keep Out" but found none. He didn't see Tom's car, either. Obviously, there was nowhere to park at the entrance to the trail.

"Let me out with the boys, Ed. See if you can locate Tom's car further down the road, and park the Land Rover nearby," said Owain. "Then you can come back and help us locate Tom and Gwyneth."

The boys and Owain grabbed the gear and started down the soggy trail. Ed drove on to find a place to park the Land Rover. Owain searched for footprints, but after the heavy rain there were none. The babbling brook had turned into a roaring stream, and in many places it had gone over its banks.

Owain told the boys, John and Tim, to look around and to call out if they found any sign of the missing couple. Meanwhile, Owain continued to move on ahead. Tim looked worried and glanced over at Owain—he didn't like this place, he said. John added that it was filled with "fairies and evil spirits." Owain told them both not to be so silly. They were not little boys but grown men, and should not worry about childish ideas. But he realized that even in this day and age superstitions still existed here in Wales.

"Come on, put your superstitions behind you, lads, we are here to find two lost friends," called out Owain as he continued down the soggy trail.

Ed caught up with them, and told Owain that he had located Tom's car parked in a turnout a short way down the road. Ed also was not happy to be in this restricted area. He was still concerned about the authorities. But after walking for a quarter of a mile, Ed spotted fresh footprints that lead off the main trail—the soft mud on the unused trail showed two sets of footprints, a man and a woman's.

Ed announced, "They went up here."

Owain examined the prints and agreed with Ed. The group headed off onto the side trail. Farther down the unused trail,

Owain spotted a rope dangling off a rock ledge above on the side of the hill.

Owain called out, "Tom! Gwyneth! Are you up there?" Immediately, two heads peered over the edge of the ledge. "Yes, thank God you found us," called down Tom.

"Stay where you are," ordered Owain, "I'm climbing up to give you a hand down. Ed, you and the lads stay here. I'm going to climb up with an extra rope. If they're hurt they may need assistance coming back down."

As Owain reached the edge of the rocky outcrop, he could see Gwyneth and Tom huddled together in a dry area towards the back part of the ledge with some covering to shield them from the storm. The couple had realized that they could not make it back down without help. Tom motioned for Owain to crawl towards him and to help Gwyneth down. He told Owain in a serious voice that he urgently needed to speak with him after she had gone.

"First, lower Gwyneth and I will have the men take her back to Gorwyn Hall. She is chilled through to the bone and could be on the edge of hypothermia," said Tom. "She wasn't prepared for this cold storm."

"You must stay here with me. We can go back in my car," Tom said to Owain. Tom gave Gwyneth a big hug. They both helped Gwyneth to the edge, and lowered her to the group below. Owain called out, "Take Gwyneth back to the hall." Soon John and Tim, with Ed in the lead, were carrying Gwyneth away.

"Okay Tom! What is this about?" demanded Owain.

Tom looked over at Owain and said. "Are you ready for a grisly sight? We must crawl back under the ledge. Watch out for the rats. Cover your head and face. We will be crawling for more than one hundred feet to reach the cave opening. I have Gwyneth's camera and here is her torch," Tom said. "Be prepared for not pretty sight."

Emerging from a narrow opening on to a small rock shelf which looked down upon the interior of a large cave, they flashed the beams from their torches around the shocking scene on the cave floor. Two bodies were lying face down, and skeleton bones lay nearby. The bodies had some flesh and cloth material on them. The rats had been busy. Owain asked for Tom's camera, and started recording the grisly scene—not a very pleasant task.

"Did you find another entrance to this place?" asked Owain over his shoulder.

"To tell you the truth, I didn't look for one. I was afraid Gwyneth would see this, so I returned to the covered ledge where you found us. There must be an opening down below," he explained.

"We need to return to Gorwyn Hall and contact the authorities immediately. You go first, Tom, and I will follow. Also, I want to take pictures of the hiking trail entrance and document the fact that there were no signs posted to keep people away from entering the trail. This is a restricted area, I am told," explained Owain. The men scrambled out of the tunnel, down to the trail, and back to Tom's parked car.

At Gorwyn Hall, Gwyneth had been put to bed under heavy wool blankets, and was sipping hot broth. Aunt Catherine gave her a sedative, so that after eating Gwyneth might fall comfortably asleep. When Tom arrived, he could check on her, and decide whether or not to call a doctor.

Downstairs in the library, Owain was on the phone to Scotland Yard. He requested that nobody bother him for any reason. Catherine tried to bring him tea and scones, but Owain firmly asked her to leave. Hywel had made himself a drink in the drawing room. Aunt Catherine scolded him about doctor's orders. Hywel had a heart attack recently. Then he turned and made her a drink also. Both sat in front of the large fireplace, wondering what had happened on the hiking trail. Ed and his sons took off once Gwyneth was safely taken into Gorwyn Hall. Tom came down, after looking in on Gwyneth and asked for something to eat. They all proceeded to the dining room, and Elena the cook brought in a tureen of fresh lamb stew, her specialty. Owain joined them in a few minutes, gobbled down his bowl of stew, and without saying anything about his phone call, asked Tom to join him in the library.

Previously, Tom and Owain had been inspectors for Scotland Yard together. They were old friends, and had worked on cases near Shrewsbury. Recently, after resigning from his post at the Yard, Tom had taken the position of manager at The Ormes Victoria Hotel on the coast of north Wales. A few months before that, Gwyneth Lydley and Tom Lewis were married at a grand wedding back in Michigan where her parents and brother, Guy lived. Guy had just gone through a terrible trial in which he had been accused of murder and involvement in drug dealing. Tom, his new brother-in-law, and Owain caught the actual criminals and brought them to justice in London. The Lydley family in America and here in England traced their descendants to Welsh knights who, during the fourteenth century, had maintained the guardianship of a religious relic secretly hidden in a chapel.

Upon returning to Wales after their honeymoon, Gwyneth and Tom moved into a cottage on the hotel's property. Gwyneth was taking classes at university in North Wales.

As Tom entered, Owain stood looking out of the large lead-framed glass windows at the lush green hillsides where the sheep were munching away on the fresh rain-drenched grass. This pleasant picture brought back memories of his boyhood summers spent here at Gorwyn Hall. Now, this ugly crime scene in the cave with the bodies and bones came before his eyes as he speculated on what acts of violence had been committed there, and when and why.

Tom, his good friend, was trying to piece together the ungodly idea of someone leaving the remains of people dumped in a cave. Not just once perhaps, but maybe many times over the years. Could there be some evil cult out there sacrificing people? The Welsh had for centuries been accused of witchcraft. But such a thing was unimaginable in this day and age. The present day Druid young people were a bunch of romantic mystics not given to sacrifices.

"Well, Tom can you give me some help before I have to return to the Yard tonight?" asked Owain. "I have spoken to Chief Superintendent William Gordon, whose voice over the phone showed immediate concern. I sent the photos from your camera to his private computer's secure site. He wants me to return to a meeting of various government officials right away. They need to organize the investigations. Do you think anyone else has seen the scene in the cave and not report it to the police?" This would be very unusual but it could have happened that people have not been in the cave recently except the criminals. The local police headquarters must be notified. Stuart, Gordon's staff man may have called them already.

"I am the only one that I know of. Gwyneth knows there are bodies, but that is all. She will say nothing if I ask her not to," said Tom. "Your aunt and uncle might have heard stories, maybe?"

"It is of the utmost importance that Gwyneth not be brought into this—or my aunt and uncle. You, on the other hand, will be questioned and asked to give a statement. The investigators must be told that your wife did not go into or near the cave. You do understand that the press will be all over this gruesome story," Owain explained. "Now, I must gather up my things and say goodbye to my aunt and uncle before I return to London."

Owain stood up and shook his good friend's hand, and left to pack his bags and would leave soon.

Tom stayed in the library for a few minutes to think over the details of what he had seen, and taken pictures of, in the cave. As he walked back into the drawing room to join Uncle Hywel and Aunt Catherine, he thought about Gwyneth upstairs. Hopefully she would be well enough to return with him tomorrow to the hotel and their little cottage before the police arrived.

"Owain requested that we not ask him any questions about the accident today," announced Hywel. Catherine was very sad that the plans for the weekend had to change. She watched Owain , her nephew, head his new Bentley down the driveway back to the main road, and on to London. Since his promotion, he found very little time to come to his boyhood home in Wales. Sadly, she turned away from the window, and went in to join her brother and Tom for some supper.

Chief Inspector
Wallon's Car Accident

Owain headed his new car towards London while gazing out at the hills that he had hiked through as a boy. This area of Wales—Snowdonia—was special to him. As the pleasant memories returned, he decided to take a short detour on one of the narrow country roads before returning to London. Just a short side trip, he told himself. As he rounded a bend in the road, he heard a thunderous booming sound coming from his right which shook the road. Immediately afterwards, there appeared a cloud of dust followed by rocks and boulders crashing down onto the road. A large one smashed into the side of Owain's Bentley, pushing the car off towards the other side of the road and down the low embankment. As the car rolled over and over with the boulders bumping and banging against the driver's side, Owain slumped over the steering wheel and went unconscious. The airbags had released and saved his life.

In a few minutes, two men climbed down and appeared over the top of the car and found Owain inside, bleeding from a head wound and unconscious.

"Leave him be," said one of the men. "We can call the constable from town, and sound like a couple of tramps." "If you say so, mate," replied the other man. The two men grabbed their bikes and headed away.

The constable of the village of Pendol received a garbled phone call from one of the men about a car in trouble off the road. He gave directions to the location of the accident, which the constable had trouble hearing. He climbed into his car went out to check the location that the caller had mumbled about.

Up ahead, he saw boulders blocking the road; and off the road, down an embankment, a car was lying on its side. "Mercy me, what has happened here?" The constable stopped his car, and proceeded to call in the car's license plate numbers. Then he climbed down to the car and found the unconscious Owain pinned behind the steering wheel. The constable made his way back up to his car and called for emergency help. The nearby police station reported that the vehicle was registered to Chief Inspector Owain Wallon of Scotland Yard. The constable reported that there was a man trapped in the vehicle, and he thought that it might be chief inspector Wallon.

With sirens blaring, an ambulance and several police cars made for the accident scene.

"Oh, my God!" shouted out a medical emergency team member. "Do you realize who this is?"

"Can you get him out safely?" Sgt. Wilson asked. The medical team requested help and a helicopter to take the badly injured man immediately to hospital. Several policemen went down to secure the vehicle from moving while they gingerly checked for a broken neck; they then strapped Owain onto a padded stretcher. Gently, keeping him as level as possible, the medical team brought Owain up to the ambulance. Sgt. Wilson stepped forward and directed the ambulance driver to an open field down the road where a helicopter was arriving.

Back at Scotland Yard in London, the sergeant on duty took the call about the accident and notified his superior.

"Good Lord! Have him brought to St. Mary's in London immediately. They have the best neurological team." Putting the phone down, Chief Superintendent Gordon told his wife that he must leave for hospital. "Call Gerald Hadley. Will you, dear? Have him meet me at St. Mary's. Chief Inspector Owain Wallon has been seriously injured with head wounds by a rock slide in Wales that hit his car. Terrible, terrible! Bye, I'm on my way." Gordon ran from their house in haste.

The corridors of St.Mary's were filled with families of patients. It was a busy Saturday night. One of Sir Gordon's office aids, Stuart, was waiting for him as Gordon entered the neurological section.

"Stuart, how is Owain?"

"He is still unconscious, sir. They have prepped him at this moment, and will take him to surgery soon," said Stuart.

"How about his family, has anyone spoken to them?"

"Yes sir, we reached his uncle at Gorwyn Hall," answered Stuart.

A Scotland Yard sergeant approached and told them that Tom Lewis was on his way to London and would represent the family. He requested to speak with Sir William Gordon. Nodding, Sir Gordon understood the reason for Tom Lewis's request.

"Stuart, check on Wallon's briefcase and suitcase, will you? He was carrying important information," said Sir Gordon. "We need those reports. If they are at the local police station in Wales, send someone from my office to retrieve the briefcase and Owain's other belongings, and bring them back to me."

"Yes, sir, right away." Stuart turned and left just as Gerald Hadley was walking in. He was recently retired from his position at the Yard. William and Gerald had been good friends at the Yard in earlier days. They talked over the developments that Owain had reported to Gordon before his accident. It was decided that Inspector Louis Duvrey was the only detective inspector without a case at this time. Neither William nor Gerald thought that he was a good choice. Most of Duvrey's cases had been in London. They both knew that there had been disappointment on the part of Inspector Duvrey, as he had been passed over when Owain Wallon was appointed Chief Inspector upon Hadley's retirement. Duvery had confidently expected to replace Gerald Hadley at the time.

Duvrey's mother was known to have connections at court as well as other high places. She and her connections had decided that a career at the Yard would be just as good for Louis as a lower position in the Foreign Office.

"Monday morning, I will inform him of his new assignment in Wales. If he does well with this assignment, he can expect a promotion, I expect," commented Sir Gordon.

On Sunday, Owain's aunt and uncle spent the day at Owain's bedside, hoping that he would regain consciousness. Tom had returned to The Ormes Victoria Hotel. Gwyneth was back helping out at the reception desk. A mist had moved in, and the few weekend guests were packing up to leave. The season was slow, but they could use this time to finish redecorating all the rooms. Tom called the hospital for news about Owain's condition. He had talked with Sir William Gordon and had gone over every detail that he could remember about that dreadful scene in the cave.

Inspector Louis Duvrey accepted his new assignment in good humor. The thought of going to Wales to investigate a cave with skeletons and bodies amused him. He and his handpicked group drove down to the area Monday morning with the pictures and reports. They would save their interview with Tom Lewis until later. Previously Duvrey had gathered together his group of specialists: Bill Denton, an anthropologist, Ted Sutter, a geologist, and John Older, an archeologist. Of course, Duvrey also traveled with his reporter friend from the news media, Burt Dagart. They would make use of the local police to conduct the investigation.

Born into an old family, inspector Louis Duvrey was the distant cousin of an earl on his mother's side and a very distant cousin of a duke. Duvrey's paternal side was not discussed. Bill, Ted, and John were his buddies. And his friend from the news media, Dagart, always had a nose for a flashy item for his tabloid newspaper. He found no difficulty in embellishing a story if it meant an opportunity for front page coverage on one of the papers that carried the latest gossip.

Within two days, Inspector Duvrey and his buddies had managed to irritate and raise the temperatures of the authorities in Snowdonia and vicinity to the boiling point. Police stations' personnel had been commandeered from Bangor to Ruthin by Duvrey and his team. Since the cave was the outer chamber of an old closed gold mine, the search for the cave entrance was undertaken and located easily. Once inside, they stomped all over the ground, destroying any evidence that might explain how the bodies got there. Duvrey didn't worry about investigation procedure. He was after press recognition. Bill Denton, the anthropologist, took an interest in studying the skeletons. Ted Sutter, the geologist, hunted for evidence of recent gold mining or digging activities. The local Police were shocked at the lack of professional investigation, and would tell their superintendent when they returned. The coroner and medical examiner went to work on the two bodies. John Older, the archeologist, searched the cave for old Celtic trinkets that could be valuable. A group with signs for "saving the environment" picketed outside, and was supported by a group of hikers who wandered over to see what was going on. Quickly the newshound Burt Dagart busied himself interviewing everyone he could. Facts were not important to him—opinions and impressions were the scoop for a story.

"Was this an old burial ground or a place for Druid sacrifices?" asked Dagart, the sly reporter. By the time he had finished interviewing all the picketers and hikers, he figured that he had his front page story with all the gory details and evil ideas that he could come up with as well as the interest of the environmental groups.

With an act of showmanship by Duvrey and Dagart who used his camera to photograph the scene of the two bodies when they are removed to the morgue, they left. The skeletons had been wrapped in blankets from the boot of their car and were to be taken to university for study. Ted, the geologist, had a box filled with stone samples which were gathered from various parts of the mine for further examination. Policemen from several police stations, who had been standing around, essentially not being used but there for effect, were sent back to their police stations. From their observation this had been very badly handled and they would report this to their commander.

Inspector Duvrey and his buddies headed for a pub that had been recommended to them by London friends. As it turned out there was only one pub they could find and it was located near Tom Lewis's new job after he left the Yard. Tomorrow Duvrey and his buddies would investigate the bodies that had been sent to the morgue. Duvrey and the others made for the The Ormes Victoria Hotel to register and planned on questioning Tom about the cave crime scene.

Tom Lewis was not overjoyed when he realized that the Duvrey's contingent was going to stay in his hotel. That evening, Duvrey and his friends started their interrogation of Tom, who managed to maintain his composure and even offered the group drinks on the house. Quite inebriated, the good old boys later stumbled up to bed to sleep it off, and Tom returned his cottage to relate to Gwyneth his experiences with the Duvrey group.

At St. Mary's Hospital in London, Owain regained consciousness and the doctors' tested their patient immediately to determine the extent of the injuries suffered by his brain. To their great surprise, they found he could pass the most difficult tasks and mental tests that they gave him. He was, thankfully, in great condition and had come through the ordeal intact both mentally and physically. Owain was to be kept under observation for twenty-four hours, and then released. They encouraged Owain to rest for the next week or two.

For Chief Superintendent William Gordon, the news coming over the air waves and in the news media was shocking. The London tabloids were carrying the front page story from north Wales about skeletons and bodies found in an old gold mine. Dagart had photographs and a very gruesome description of the cave, plus photos of the environmentalist protesters (and their statements) to capture the bizarre interests of his readers. Included was a statement by Inspector Duvrey about his excellent investigation of the crime scene. Normally, the Yard never sought publicity when investigating a crime scene.

Superintendent Gordon did not respond to phone calls from the press. His staff told the press that they had no statement to make at this time, since the criminal investigation was ongoing. Orders were put out for Duvrey to return to headquarters at once.

Unfortunately, before Duvrey could be reached, he had made one more dramatic thrust to create news in the little village of Dewi Sant. The bodies of the two people found in the cave had been identified at the morgue. They died of natural causes and had been buried in a local family plot on a section of land recently purchased by Dirk Otis Shedweld, a wealthy businessman from Liverpool. When he purchased the property, his solicitor was assured that these graves in the old family plot could be moved down to the graveyard in the village near the church of Dewi Sant.

Quite a sum of money for the local school was donated by the new owner of the land, and the solicitor told his client that everything was satisfactory. Construction on Shedweld's country house could begin immediately. The original owners of the land had moved to Australia. Their descendents were very happy to sell; and stop paying the high taxes on the property. Six coffins and their occupants were to be moved at a cost to be paid by the new owners. The vicar of the church had made arrangements for a service of re-internment to be conducted. The lovely country house was built, and everyone was happy. They thought.

Inspector Duvrey paid a visit to Shedweld and explained that the bodies in the cave had been identified with the records of two of the people who were buried originally on his property. Therefore, something was amiss, as Duvrey pointed out with his best public-school demeanor. He wanted to tentatively confide in Dirk Otis Shedweld that he, Duvrey was open to a reimbursement .Of course, his pet news reporter, Burt Dagart, was standing nearby with pen and pad ready. Shedweld took Duvrey aside and Burt Dagart discretely moved closer to listen to them discussing something about a business proposition, and from what he thought he heard, it appeared to be a scheme of some sort. Then, they shook hands. Dagart suspected his boss was up to something, and he was going to make sure it included him.

Shortly afterward, the village constable, Jimmy Morton, came up to Duvrey while he was in conversation with Burt Dagart. "Sir, Scotland Yard is in need of speaking with you, right away, sir."

"Oh dear, my cell phone battery is low. Forgot to charge the damn thing last night." He turned to the reporter. "Say, old boy, can I use yours to call the Yard?"

After Duvrey spoke with Sir Gordon, he knew the number one plan for his publicity shot was over. Superintendent Gordon told him that he had broken a hard and fast rule when he sought recognition by the press. Duvrey must return to London immediately for a reprimand. That would be alright Duvrey thought. He had a number two plan with Shedweld.

In the meantime, Owain was recovering at his new place in London. While he watched news reports on the tellie while holding copies of the London papers on his lap. Then the telephone rang.

"Owain, I have just spoken to your doctors, and they tell me that you are well enough to come in tomorrow morning to my office. We need you back on the case," said Sir Gordon in a distinct-ly strained voice. "I realize that this is asking much of you after your accident. We will make sure you receive all the help that you need and we'll pay any expenses that you find necessary in handling this case, old boy."

After hanging up the phone, Owain sat back with the newspa-pers—and the phone rang again. It was Aunt Catherine, who sus-pected rightly, after reading the newspaper, suspected that Gordon would want Owain back to handle the case. However, she wanted him to come to Gorwyn Hall, and not to go into the office at least for a month. Owain realized that she would be upset when she heard the news that he must take over the case again. His aunt could not be stopped from calling Sir Gordon, Owain was sure, and she'd complain to him that it was too soon after the accident. She had his best interests at heart. He decided for now he would have to reassure her, but still return to the case in Wales.

Again the phone rang, and this time it was Tom Lewis. An hour after talking with Tom concerning Duvrey's poor handling of the investigation, Owain knew he needed a good night's rest before he left in the morning. Duvrey, this time, had really bungled the investigation. Duvrey's poor mother, whom everyone knew to be a gracious lady and very well regarded by old British society, had had her hands full with this arrogant twerp of a son. Now, her son had seriously damaged the credibility of Scotland Yard.

Promptly the next morning, Owain left for Sir William Gor-don's office at the Yard. Inspector Duvrey's conduct had left a stain on the reputation of the special investigative branch of Scot-land Yard. All the officers knew that they were never to discuss a case with the press or to allow unofficial photographs to be taken and then shown on the front page of the tabloids. It was a seri-ous breach of security and conduct. Louis Duvrey, upon being dis-missed by Sir Gordon, went straight to his mother's place in the countryside to explain the regrettable situation. She had gone to great lengths using her connections to have him placed at Scot-land Yard. This turn of events by her only child brought her to despair. Lord Peter Whitecoft, an old friend, called Lady Duvrey to extend his condolences for her son's regrettable behavior. But Du-vrey had no intention of being "put down." He had a new scheme and a business adventure in mind thanks to his handshake with Shedweld.

After leaving the chief superintendent's office, Owain went back to his own office to gather up his things and leave for Wales. Somehow he would have to explain to Aunt Catherine that he could not stay at Gorwyn Hall. He was on serious official business, and the details of this case must be cleared up as soon as possible with discretion and the least amount of publicity. Detective Sergeant Clyde McDowell would accompany him. He was a good solid investigator, and discreet, and Owain was pleased that McDowell had been assigned to him to assist in the investigation. In the past McDowell had shown excellent skills and would soon be promoted, Owain was sure. He had not worked any cases with Wallon before, but his record showed that he was an outstanding investigator.

Arrangements were made for them to stay in a small hotel near the district's police headquarters. Upon arriving, he and Sgt. Mc-Dowell made their way to the station and presented their credentials to District Superintendent Edwin Cadwell. The atmosphere was decidedly unfriendly and strained. However, by the time Wallon and McDowell had left, everyone was relaxed and ready to help. The police department's ruffled pride had been put aside.

The next stop on Owain's agenda was to talk with Tom Lewis, who was waiting for them at the hotel, and they followed him into his office. Owain explained that they could not stay at The Ormes Victoria but must be near the district police station. Tom understood. Even though he welcomed his friend, Owain to stay at the hotel, he realized that Owain had to work with the local police.

Sgt. McDowell took copious notes at each stop. It was late in the day by the time they left Tom Lewis. Sgt. McDowell suggested that they might have supper in the pub near their hotel. McDowell suggested that it might be a good idea to make a friendly gesture. Owain agreed. As they entered the pub, the owner was not sure how to greet the two officials from Scotland Yard, but when one of the local sergeants came up to them with a friendly greeting, the owner gave them a friendly smile as well.

Over dinner and a couple pints of ale, Owain and McDowell discussed the events of the day. The local police stations were handled very diplomatically by Chief Inspector Wallon. The police superintendents in Bangor and Ruthin had been appeased by Wallon's Welsh background and by his attitude towards the case. They no longer felt threatened by the intrusions of the aristocratic bearing of Inspector Duvrey and they were willing to give Wallon the full cooperation of their departments. Owain was pleased. This was a big hurdle to have overcome.

Tomorrow, he and Sgt. McDowell would visit the morgue and take a better look at the two bodies that had been removed from the cave. Then, they would visit the village that recently had given permission for the removal of several coffins from the private property of a wealthy businessman, and their reinterment in the graveyard at the church in Dewi Sant. Also, first thing in the morning, Owain wanted to return to the cave site to review what had occurred there. He was thinking that he would like to bring in his own specialists in the fields of archeology, geology, and anthropology. With a long day ahead of them, the two men headed up to their rooms for the night.

III

Investigation of Lost Cave

Early in the morning, Sgt. McDowell and Chief Inspector Wallon picked up Detective Sgt. Floyd Jones, who had been assigned to the case by Superintendent Cadwell from the regional police station in North Wales. Sgt. McDowell drove directly out to the cave entrance sight. Already the workmen were cleaning up the area, and had started boarding up the entrance when their police car arrived. Detective Sgt. Jones handed the foreman of the work detail an order explaining that the entrance was not to be closed off until the officers from Scotland Yard had a chance to investigate inside. Wallon, with his waders on, proceeded to enter the cold, damp cave, followed by Sgt. McDowell and Det. Sgt. Jones.

Using their torches, they made their way into the large open area where the bodies had been found, along with the skeletons. Footprints were everywhere and all of them appeared to be freshly made. Owain aimed the beam from his torch upwards to see if he could spot the opening for the tunnel where he and Tom had looked down on the gruesome sight of bodies and skeletons on the cave floor. He thought he had found the opening when McDowell came up behind him and asked, "Did you locate something, sir?"

"I am not sure, McDowell. Can you see an opening up there where I am pointing the beam from my torch? Tom and I took pictures of this scene last Sunday," said Owain. "Take out your camera with the flash, and point it in that direction up there. We can check the pictures later, on the computer. This place has been completely disturbed—look at all these footprints. Go ahead and take more pictures, anyway. We can compare them with the ones I took before. Then, I want to walk down the tunnels and check to see if I can find evidence of what that geologist of Duvrey's, Ted Sutter, had been doing. We mustn't waste too much time here. Whatever evidence that was here before, has been seriously disturbed by Duvrey's men walking around the area."

After speaking with the foreman about constructing a door with a padlock over the entrance, they left in the chief inspector's car. The next stop would be the morgue where the bodies from the cave had been taken. The investigation needed to establish certain facts concerning the condition of the bodies and a possible date of death, as well as when they had been first interred in the ground before being removed to the cave.

The mortuary technician was very helpful. Fingerprints were taken and pictures sent out for identification. The male and female bodies were found to be listed in the official bureau of death records as having died ten years earlier. Decomposition had of course taken place, and matched the time period of ten years. As in most burials, the bodies had been protected by coffins. There were no coffins found in the cave, though. The morgue technician told them that it appeared that the man and woman had probably died of natural causes, as listed on the death certificates. So, with a copy of these death certificates in hand, Chief Inspector Wallon, Sgt. McDowell, and District Inspector Jones headed out to the village of Dewi Sant, where the bodies had been originally buried. This was the same village that Duvrey and his friends had visited just before being ordered to return to London.

Since it was lunch time, Wallon suggested stopping at a country pub to have something to eat on the way. It was while having their lunch that Detective Sgt. Jones commented to Chief Inspector Wallon, "Sir, excuse me, when I was with the previous Scotland Yard inspector Duvrey and his group of professors, I noticed several odd things that had taken place."

"Oh, yes, and what were they?" Wallon asked.

"Well, sir, it seemed to me that there had been on the floor at the side of the cave interior, the distinct imprints of two boxes which were then trampled on by people walking around inside the cave. Also, we did notice old footprints. No one seemed to think that the footprints were important and all the walking around caused the imprints to be destroyed. No one seemed at all interested in footprints at the time. The archeologist, John Older, bent over one of the dead bodies, and then put something in his pocket. He did not have an evidence bag with him. Then he walked over to the other fellow, the anthropologist named Bill Denton, while he was examining the skeletons, and removed one of the skulls from the ground. Right then, the man they referred to as a geologist called over to the other two men to give him a hand with the large heavy bags he had collected while searching the tunnels. There were three bags, and each man took one to the car. Shortly after that, Inspector Duvrey and the news photographer went out to talk with the small crowd of hikers and picketers to confirm their worst fears—that the cave had been vandalized by outsiders and that this was an evil deed. He especially emphasized the word 'evil.' Then Inspector Duvrey and his associates returned to their car and drove off."

"Bags of what, Jones?" asked Sgt. McDowell.

"I don't know. They looked heavy, though. Oh, I forgot—and the skeletons were gathered up and placed in blankets that they had in their car," said Sgt. Jones. "That is not a professional way of handling evidence, I would say, sir."

"McDowell, make note of all that Sergeant Jones has told us; and we will have to follow up on these items, but not today. Thank you, Sergeant Jones, for coming forward with what you observed. This is all very important to the case," said Wallon in a serious tone.

When they arrived at the village graveyard near the church, Owain observed a crowd of people standing around. Village constable Jimmy Morton approached the police car.

"Something very strange has happened to the two graves in our church graveyard where the missing bodies were supposed to have been buried, sir. Both grave sites were dug up recently—last night," he said. "The people in the village of Dewi Sant are very upset."

Chief Inspector Wallon left the car, and immediately went over to see the place for himself. McDowell and the detective sergeant from north Wales's headquarters quickly followed. They could see that two large holes the sizes of coffins were sitting open by the two headstones. Wallon asked the constable to move the people down to the church and that he would speak with them soon. While the group of villagers left for the church, McDowell and Jones carefully searched the area. Yellow tape and stakes were erected to protect the scene from further disturbances. Chief Inspector Wallon and the constable headed over to the church to speak with the villagers.

The local citizens were clustered together in a group near the front of the church. Their vicar was speaking to them when Wallon walked down the aisle.

"Please, Inspector," said the vicar. "The people of this—"

The constable Morton interrupted the vicar. "This is Chief Inspector Wallon, vicar."

"Forgive me, I stand corrected, the other gentleman was Inspector Duvrey, I believe?"

Wallon introduced himself to Father Daniel and the village people. "I have been assigned to this case. Inspector Duvrey, who was here recently, has left for London on a personal matter. We will do our best to resolve this unfortunate situation as quickly as we can. Sergeants McDowell and Jones are at this moment searching the area for evidence of whom—and when—someone desecrated your families' graveyard. If you saw anything, heard anything, or know who was digging last night, please speak with us. As you may already know, there are two bodies in the mortuary that have been identified as once having been buried in the place where the grave stones are. We are certain from the records that they died of natural causes, and were originally buried near here.

"The deceased's coffins were to be moved to this graveyard along with others from their family. For reasons that we have not been able to ascertain, two of the bodies were left in a cave, but without coffins. We understand that the original family that owned the land and their family's small cemetery on it left this area for Australia about eight years ago. Their land was recently purchased by a gentleman from Liverpool. He went through the correct procedure to move the coffins from the small cemetery to the main cemetery in the village of Dewi Sant near this church. We understand the vicar of this church and the people of the village were in agreement with this move. We are here to assist the district police headquarters with their investigation. Therefore, we ask you again, please come forward and speak to one of us if you have information about this case. Thank you."

Chief Inspector Wallon went over to speak with the vicar privately. Most of the town's people who gathered were talking amongst themselves when one of the men came up to Wallon and Father Daniel.

"Sir, some of us did hear noises last night after midnight; I guess we ignored them for various reasons. Since the noise came from the graveyard, we were not keen on going out there in the middle of the night to investigate, if you know what I mean, sir. We thought the village constable should do it."

"Just a minute Pete—I am a sound sleeper; no one called me to report anything until this morning," said Constable Morton defensively.

Sgt. McDowell and Sgt. Jones came up just then and McDowell announced, "Sir, we have searched the area for footprints, and bagged a little evidence. However, most of the ground was trampled. We did find tire marks, and some other marks that looked like two very heavy objects which had been dragged toward the vehicle that left the tire marks. I have taken pictures of the marks."

"I see," said Wallon. "Could those marks have been made by heavy coffins that were taken from the freshly dug grave holes?"

"Why, yes, sir, I guess that is a possibility," said McDowell.

"At this point, we should return with Sergeant Jones and speak to his district superintendent. Thank you for your time, vicar. Constable Morton, would you talk with the people here, and send us a report concerning what they heard and maybe saw last night?"

At headquarters, they entered the station and went to Superintendent Cadwell's office. He was waiting for them and had a sergeant bring in tea. As they sat down, Supt. Cadwell told Wallon that Sir William Gordon had called. Evidently, the doctors were worried about Wallon's accident injures. He was still recovering from a serious head wound he had received in the car accident. As Cadwell looked over at Wallon, he confirmed in his mind the doctors' concerns. They sat discussing the case and Wallon decided that at this juncture he could leave Sgt. McDowell behind to work with Supt. Cadwell and Detective Jones, and he would take a few days off. Superintendent Cadwell assured Owain that as head of the police district, he was a competent and experienced officer, and could be trusted to take over the investigation until the chief inspector's return.

"My aunt Catherine at Gorwyn Hall has reported her concerns to the doctors, I'm sure. She is a very caring person, and I probably should spend some time letting her nurse me along, so to speak. The accident occurred a little over a week ago," said Wallon.

"Aye, then, thee be one of us," Cadwell said in Welsh as a show of comradeship with Owain.

"Alright, McDowell, I'm ready to follow the doctor's orders. You can drive me over in the Land Rover to Gorwyn Hall."

The drive was through a beautiful countryside. McDowell commented to his boss that he had not realized how attractive this area of Wales was. Everyone always thought Wales was nothing but coal mines with ugly slag heaps left behind. McDowell's family was from Scotland. His comment brought a smile to Owain's tired face.

Owain looked out the car window, and realized that he, too, had taken the beauty of Snowdonia for granted. London and all its cultural events, plays and shows, and night life had been a part of his life these recent years. He had spent hours at the British Museum, and at the many art gallery openings he loved to attend. Then, there were the crime, murder, and drugs cases which were a part of his job. Coming back to Wales on this case reminded him of another case he had had in Shropshire. His mind drifted off until McDowell made the turn into the driveway to Gorwyn Hall. Even with the drizzling rain, and the weather a bit gloomy, the place was a welcome sight to Owain. Aunt Catherine greeted them at the open front door. The two old sheep dogs were standing beside her, wagging their tails. Owain stepped out of the car and spoke to McDowell before he grabbed his suitcase and went in. He had already collected his things from the hotel, and McDowell was to keep the Land Rover from Yard Headquarters and continue working on the investigation.

"I will expect a report from you daily, McDowell. Superintendent Cadwell has assured me that he assigned Sergeant Jones to stay on the case," said Owain.

"Yes, sir," answered McDowell. "You can depend on me."

The evening was chilly with the mist sinking down onto the hills as Owain entered the old hall with suitcase and briefcase in hand. Elena, the cook, sent her daughter Angie to collect Owain's bags and take them up to his room. Sitting in the comfortable drawing room, Hywel waited for Owain and Catherine to join him. Hywel fondly greeted his nephew. "You look tired, my boy. . . . Come in and have a drink. We will be going in to dinner later."

"I will join you shortly. Mix my usual, while I go to my room for a minute to clean up," said Owain as he headed for the grand oak stairway.

"He does look pale and tired," Hywel commented to Catherine, who also looked concerned.—

In his room, Owain sighed and realized his head wound was throbbing. Sir Gordon was right to force him to take some time off from the case. Sgt. McDowell and Sgt. Jones were certainly competent enough to continue without him for a few days.

This bedroom had been his boyhood retreat when he had needed time to recover from exams during his university days. As he gazed out the window towards the mist-covered hills with all the familiar images of his childhood, all the memories of his time here at Gorwyn Hall came flooding back.

He had been very fortunate to survive the car accident that killed his parents when he was five, but that dreadful time had never left him. He vaguely remembered his mother, Elizabeth, the older sister of Aunt Catherine and Uncle Hywel. His father was Edward Wallon. Owain wanted to know who his father had been. Who were the Wallons? Why didn't anyone want to talk about them? While away at university, he had searched for someone with the last name of Wallon but found no one who knew of his father. He thought that this was odd because he knew that his father had been educated at university, but he did not know which one. Owain turned from the window and went downstairs to join his aunt and uncle. Owain decided that whatever the reason might be, he felt that someday someone would speak to him about his father.

In the morning, Owain joined his aunt and uncle for their morning walk about the hills around Gorwyn Hall. He enjoyed the country air and exercise. Just to be in the company of his family and dogs were enough.

After a couple of days of quiet rest and Elena's cooking, he looked forward to returning to the case. Sgt. McDowell had been sending him reports every day by courier. It was now apparent that the bodies found in the cave had been removed from the coffins during the reburial period in the church graveyard. Something had been placed in the coffin in the deceased person's place before reburial occurred. No one in the village had suspected foul play at the time. Owain wondered what it was that was put in the coffins in place of the bodies. Whoever it was had to have taken the coffins to the cave with the bodies still inside them. They then removed the bodies, left them on the cave floor, and placed something else in the coffins. They reburied the coffins in the graveyard without anyone realizing what had happened. Once the bodies were discovered in the cave, they then had to rush over to the graveyard in Dewi Sant and dig up the graves again and remove the coffins to be hidden elsewhere. This time they caught the attention of some of the villagers during the night. Why did they have to vandalize this old cave in the first place? The answers must involve the cave. Could there be artifacts from historic times that could bring good prices on the illegal markets? Stolen Celtic pieces sold for high prices if they were made of gold. Was there someone in the village involved in the grave-robbing business? He and McDowell—plus Jones—should investigate this possibility.

Coffins and Murder in the Bay

A call came into Supt. Cadwell's office reporting that two fishermen had watched as unidentified men pushed what looked like two coffins over the side of a small boat into the water of the bay the previous night. Cadwell sent a police launch out to investigate. They found that the coffins were lying in deep water. No effort was made to retrieve the coffins by the police launch. They told Cadwell that it would take diving equipment to retrieve them from the bottom of the bay. Cadwell decided to leave the coffins where they were for the time being if he needed to retieve them at all. He planned to let Sgt. Jones know when he came in for duty.

In the meantime, Sgt. McDowell had contacted the computer specialists in the Special Branch of the Yard's offices to track down the records of the wealthy businessman who had bought the land and built a very large cottage on the property. The cottage owner, Dirk Otis Shedweld from Liverpool, had several businesses licensed under his name. Some of the businesses were also licensed in Sydney, Australia. One was a mining company; another was a salvage yard business, and the third one was a geological firm that searched for rare metal deposits. All this information was very interesting, Owain thought when he read McDowell's report. Ted Sutter, the geologist Duvrey had used as part of his team to investigate the cave, turned out to be an employee of Mr. Shedweld's geology firm.

An early morning phone call came at Gorwyn Hall for Chief Inspector Wallon. Angie ran up the stairs to knock on Owain's door.

He glanced at his watch, grabbed his robe, and headed downstairs to the telephone.

"Hello!"

"Sir, it's McDowell here. There has been a murder. One of the workmen who worked for the construction company when Mr. Dirk Otis Shedweld built his cottage was found floating in the bay. We can't locate the archeologist, John Older, or the anthropologist, Bill Denton; and we think that the geologist, Ted Sutter, is hiding out with friends. The people at Mr. Shedweld's firm's offices gave us what information they had. Shedweld is at police headquarters speaking with Superintendent Cadwell right now. The building contractor, Conrad, is out of town and we are trying to locate him. I called our offices, and talked to Stuart, and he told me that Duvrey had left for Australia to be a clerk at our British consulate offices in Sydney."

"Alright, McDowell, I want you to bring Sergeant Jones with you, and drive up here to Gorwyn Hall. Wear hiking clothes—we are going to investigate two areas that I should have gone back to long before this."

After hanging up the phone and turning to Aunt Catherine, who was standing behind him, Owain already knew what she would have to say about his returning to work too soon.

"You know what the doctors told you. A full week and a half for rest," said his aunt firmly.

"Now, now, I promise I will take it easy. I feel much improved after resting a couple of days. Please, Aunt Catherine, at this moment I could do with some breakfast." He leaned over and kissed her cheek.

Accordingly, Owain was ready when McDowell and Jones drove up to Gorwyn Hall. On the previous day, Owain had contacted Dr. Glyn Anderson, a geologist friend whom Owain knew from his student days at Bangor University in Wales. He was much respected in his field, and specialized in the geology of the region. Glyn would meet them at the village of Pendol, near the car accident scene, with Constable Wilson.

As they drove into Pendol, Dr. Anderson and Constable Wilson were waiting for them. After a short discussion, the two police cars headed up to the location where Owain's Bentley had been shoved off the road by a rock slide. Locating a place to leave the cars, they made their way back to the location of Owain's accident. Immediately, Dr. Anderson bent over to examine the rocks that had been cleared off the road where Owain's car had been located. His car had been removed, but it was not difficult to recreate the accident site. Wilson explained to Anderson and the others what he had found when they rescued Chief Inspector Wallon from his car. Of course, Owain had been unconscious, so this reconstruction of the scene helped him review the accident again.

Dr. Anderson made his way down the slope to the large rock that had hit the car. Then he climbed back up to the road and motioned to the others to follow him up the hill in the direction of the rockslide. As they reached the top of the hill, Anderson announced that this had been no ordinary rockslide. In fact, explosives had been used here that had loosened the rocks enough to cause them to tumble down onto the road.

Dr. Anderson continued his search further back on the hill, and called out to the others.

"Come over here. This is all very interesting. An effort has been made to blast out this side of the hill. I am collecting rock samples to take back to my lab," said Anderson.

Owain ordered a search for more material evidence, footprints, and anything that might identify who had been up here using explosives. In an hour they had collected several evidence bags filled with items plus parts of the blasting caps from the explosives. As they made their way back to their cars, Owain announced that the next stop was the trail where he had rescued his two friends, Tom and Gwyneth, the day they had crawled up onto a rock ledge for shelter from the storm.

Upon returning to the main road to head north, Sgt. McDowell caught Jones by the arm and pointed to a car parked farther back on the road. The driver appeared to be watching them. Constable Wilson had noticed the car as well; Owain was busy conversing with Dr. Anderson. Wilson took out his cell and called in the license number on the car. They waited for a response. Wilson announced that the car was leased out by a rental agency in Liverpool. Constable Wilson made for his car to go and check out the driver. Upon seeing the police officers, the rental car turned and quickly drove away. Anderson, who had left his car back at the town of Pendol, climbed into the car with the officers Sgt. McDowell, Sgt. Jones, and Chief Inspector Wallon. They continued on to the next location.

The weather was holding as McDowell parked the car in the same turn-out where Tom had parked during the time when he and Gwyneth had gone hiking the day they were rescued from the ledge.

"We head this way," announced Chief Inspector Wallon. "The trail entrance is just down the road. This area is restricted, and there should be a "no entrance" sign here. When we enter on to the main trail, look for a smaller unused trail to the left—this is where Tom and his wife left the main trail."

Dr. Anderson made note of the fact that there was a missing restriction sign, and said that he would report it to the park authorities.

Walking along, Owain found the turn off, and started on to the old trail. Again, after looking off to his left and down, Owain turned to the others and said, "Look up to your left and you should see a rock outcropping and ledge."

Anderson pointed up: "There, I see it."

"We will have to climb up to that ledge to find the opening into the cave," Owain told him.

After making an arduous climb, Anderson and Wallon made it to a flat, slanted section of rock. Officers McDowell and Jones waited below, as there was not enough room on the flat rock area for all of them.

"We have to crawl under the ledge in the back as Tom and I did before," Owain said. "Now, Glyn, I want you to go first. I have been back there before. After crawling for about a hundred feet you will see an opening. It should be the opening to the cave where the skeletons and bodies were found. By the way, rats like this place," Owain warned him. "Here, take my torch. You may need two."

"Blast it all. This place is covered with rat dung," called back Glyn.

After investigating, Glyn joined Owain again on the flat rock area. "You were right; there is an opening to a big cave. I didn't see any sign of people down there. All was very quiet. However, this cave is very old; and I will need to investigate the place from the other entrance. But before we leave, over to your right, as the ledge continues on, I need to take some rock samples." Glyn pulled out tools that he had strapped to his waist, and cautiously made his way along the rocky outcrop.

Half an hour later, he returned with his small sack of rock samples, and they climbed down to join McDowell and Jones. The two detective sergeants had been scouring the area for signs of footprints further down the trail.

Back at the car, Chief Inspector Wallon was going over in his mind the possibility of going on to the cave opening today. "It is late. However, I would like to give Dr. Anderson the chance to see the old gold mine and cave." No one had had lunch. Sgt. Jones suggested that they grab some sandwiches at the country pub they had passed while driving up to the hiking trail.

After downing their sandwiches in the car, they drove to the cave entrance. Detective Jones located the key to the padlock on the makeshift door covering the boarded-up entrance. Grabbing their torches, they made their way into the cave again. Dr. Anderson, following behind, studied the rock walls. Looking closely at the markings on the walls, he stopped to study with great interest these markings. Owain reminded him that they were short on time.

As they started their investigation, Jones said he was going back to the police car for a thermos of coffee. As he approached the entrance, suddenly the wooden door was slammed shut and the padlock put in place. Jones hammered with his fist on the door and yelled out.

"Who is out there? Open this door in the name of the law."

There was no answer. Soon, he heard a car start up and drive off. Shocked, Sgt. Jones knew from the sound the engine made that it was the chief inspector's car. Returning to the others, who were running up to see what had just happened, Chief Inspector Wallon demanded to know how it was that they could be locked in. Sgt. Jones explained that he must have left the key in the padlock after opening the door. Sgt. McDowell announced that he must have left the keys in the car.

Wallon looked at both sergeants, who had guilty looks on their faces, and said, "First the rental car at the rock slides scene, and now this. I would say that there is someone out there tracking us. Cell phones won't work inside this cave."

They went up to the wooden barricade across the opening of the cave, but without heavy tools, they were at a loss how to break down the door. A crowbar was needed to break through the heavy barricade and door.

"Who would want to lock the police in this cave? This is a serious act of breaking the law," said Sgt. Jones angrily. Owain and Glyn had returned to the back of the cave to discuss the situation.

"I think I can climb up to that opening that leads to the trail we were on earlier," Glyn said.

"That's a pretty steep climb, and we didn't bring climbing equipment with us," replied Owain.

"The walls of the cave are jagged, and with some luck I can find finger holds and maneuver my way up."

"Where do you want to start?"

"How about over there? I can see a way that I can move slightly to the right along the cave wall to the opening."

Navigating his way up the rough wall, Glyn made the climb look easy. However, only an experienced climber could find just the right finger and toe holds. McDowell and Jones, who had returned to the large cave watched in amazement. Once inside the opening, Glyn turned around and called down to the others.

"I will make my way back to the road, and if my cell phone does not work when I'm out in the open I will have to hike down to the pub and call the police to come get you. If I have to wait until I reach the pub, it will be much longer before I can get help." With that Glyn climbed back into the tunnel.

"Sir, I'm sorry, I should never have been so careless," said Jones.

"Forget it, Jones. Let's see if one of these tunnels leads to another opening. There seems to be several footprints down this one. McDowell, you come with me, and Jones, you wait here. If you hear someone at the door, wait until they open it, and then make a move. Are you carrying firearms?"

"No, sir."

"Well, tackle them if you can, and put handcuffs on them; use force if you have to. Most likely the one who took the key and locked us in will return. So be ready. We will not be gone long.

Make it fifteen minutes by our watches." Owain figured that this was more of a cruel trick than a serious danger for them.

Jones looked a little uncertain as Wallon and McDowell disappeared down the dark tunnel. The search for another exit was not successful, and Wallon and MacDowell returned to find Jones standing at the cave door with a piece of board in his hands. The sound of noises outside of the door caused the two men to make haste to Jones's side.

The door swung open and the men grabbed two young boys by their collars as they were about to enter the cave. Jones and McDowell had the two boys on the floor of the cave, handcuffed, in short order.

Chief Inspector Wallon demanded to know if they knew that they were locking the door with police officers inside.

The boys were obviously traumatized. "We didn't do it," said one boy. "Some lady told us to go back here, and let you out—she gave us the key," said the other boy. Sgt. Jones began to interrogate the boys. He wrote their names and addresses down in his note pad.

"Now, tell me. Did you know this 'lady'?" asked Jones.

Both boys started talking at the same time. It seemed the boys were in the woods when a car drove up and this lady who they had seen before in the village with that group of people who want to save the forests.—She gave them the key, and a quid, and told them to come back and unlock the door at the cave entrance.

"Did she tell you that we were policemen?" asked Sgt. Jones

"No!" said the boys.

"Can you describe the car?"

Again, "No" was their answer.

In the distance they heard sirens, and then marked police cars arrived. One of Supt. Cadwell's inspectors shouted out, "What's going on? This woman drove up to the station, jumped out of *your* car and said that you were endangering the forest. She ran around the corner and jumped back in her car, and drove away. At that time, an emergency call comes in from a Dr. Glyn Anderson about you being locked in a cave."

After a few more minutes of explanation, the boys were taken home to their families, and everyone went back to police headquarters. Cadwell didn't know whether to laugh or be serious. Dr. Anderson was picked up on the road, where he had made the call to headquarters. He needed to return for his car in Pendol. Then he wanted to return to headquarters to pick up Chief Inspector Wallon and take him to his place for dinner. Owain was far from being in a good mood. However, Glyn had information for him that could shed new light on the case.

After driving over from police headquarter, Glyn and Owain climbed the stairs to Glyn's flat, located near the university in Bangor.

"Come on Owain, let's clean up and go down to my favorite pub. While we are having a nice supper, I can tell you about my geological findings and speculations. This has been a very interesting and adventurous day," said Glyn.

Owain raised himself up off of Glyn's comfortable chair and grumbled. "Good, let's go."

The two men had been friends years ago, but had not seen very much of each other lately. After they attended university ten years ago, they only had seen each other from time to time. Glyn was a tall, lanky fellow with straight blond hair down to his shoulders. He had gone on to finish his doctorate in geology, and taught here at the university. Glyn was too busy with his rocks to find a girl to put up with his jaunts out to rock piles.

At a typical university pub, they sat sipping pints of ale while they waited for their meal. Glyn spoke to his friend.

"You do know what this is all about, don't you? . . . Gold! Some amateurs, or maybe construction workers, have stumbled upon a small amount of gold, and started mucking about looking for a lost mine. The explosion up on the hill above the rock slide was an attempt to find more rocks with gold. Somehow this amateur group found a cave, and decided to hide the bodies from the coffins that were to be transferred to the village graveyard. The coffins from the graveyard transfer project that were buried without the bodies were probably filled with rocks that this group had found in the old gold mine. It would be a great hiding place for the gold, but they needed the help of a geologist to confirm that it was gold and not iron pyrites—fool's gold. Unexpectedly, Tom and you come along, and discover the bodies left in the deserted cave. Hence, they had to dig up the coffins in the graveyard containing the rocks they had collected, and drag them away to be disposed of in the bay.

"That explains part of the case. This Ted Sutter takes keen interest when these amateurs approach him with samples of their rocks. He realizes that there may be evidence of gold, and agrees to go along with Duvrey to the cave. During the time that they are in the cave, Ted takes off for the tunnels with his sacks and tools. What he found we don't know. However, when I was with you on the trail, where Tom and his wife had climbed up to the ridge for shelter from the storm, I did have a chance to search out an interesting quartz vein within bands of shale. If I am correct, there might be a small amount of gold in this quartz vein that appears near the surface, which had lain there unnoticed.

As yet, no one seems aware of this opening into the cave. The trail has been unused for. . . . who knows how long. All the interest was in the cave, and the old mining tunnel off of it. Ted Sutter is the one to locate. He probably, has some answers for you."

"That is all well and good, Glyn, but so far we have not been able to locate him. What about this female nut who locked us in the cave and drove off in a police car? Also, why would these guys go to the trouble to use a reburied coffin?" asked Owain.

"Just a guess, but I bet the environmental group that picketed the gold mine location has been watching for anyone reentering the cave. They feel that it is their duty to save the area from any further disturbance by mining. Nearby was the location of a gold mine active one hundred or so years ago. Remember, you were not wearing uniforms. The car was unmarked. So she was doing her environmental civic duty to discourage outside investment seekers.

"Now, returning to Sutter, I do know a little about this scholarly maverick. He has been rejected by the geology society for his brash attacks on their attitudes towards mining for gain. Wales has continually suffered from invaders seeking investment opportunities which have torn up this beautiful landterrain, and not made any attempt to reconstruct their disastrous destruction of mother earth's beauty. This Ted Sutter is one of a group that is interested in promoting mining. I am vehemently opposed to mining. As for the coffin transfer, convenience would be my guess."

"Well, that may be a clue to their identity. It was a good thing we brought you along."

"The young boys were sent back to let us out. This was just supposed to be a warning."

"Just a moment—who is giving us a warning?" Owain asked, giving Glyn a serious look.

Glyn carefully side-stepped the question, because he had his own thoughts about who the lady was and said, "I do have a request. I need to go back into the cave to see where Ted Sutter collected his rock samples; and I have 2 of my colleagues that I would like to bring with me."

"Arrangements can be made for you to return to the cave."

"One more problem bothers me about the objects that were taken from the cave, and the skeletons that the anthropologist took. Where are the anthropologist and archeologist that Duvrey used?" asked Glyn.

"They are both missing. One is named Bill Denton and the other is John Older. The old bones were to have been taken to a lab for study. John Older removed one of the skulls from the others, and also a small object near one of the bodies. Denton and Older need to be found and questioned."

"You have a challenging case on your hands. Do you like your career as a law enforcement officer? Seems to me, you studied for the law in university. I remember that academically you had an outstanding future," stated Glyn.

Owain explained to Glyn that he had not wanted to go into his uncle's law firm and spend the rest of his life there. Both his uncle and aunt were tremendously important to him following the death of his parents. They gave him love, support, and a wonderful home during the difficult years of his childhood. But he had wanted to step out on his own, and that of course included going to London.

"Your mother was a Gorwyn, I presume. What do you know about your father and his family, the Wallons?" Glyn asked.

"Nothing—his name and family are never brought up. As I grew older, I did try to ask about him. Uncle Hywel and Aunt Catherine seemed very reluctant to talk about the subject, and usually changed the topic. I felt that it made them feel uncomfortable and maybe unappreciated for having raised me. They blamed Father for the death of their sister Elizabeth, you see."

"You do have an aristocratic look about you. I have not seen very much of the Gorwyn family, but I remember that the lads at university used to talk about someone that you resembled. Do you have photographs of your father?" asked Glyn.

"Really? Who did they think I resembled?" asked Owain. "Some English aristocrat? Oh! Please, I don't pretend to be anything but Welsh," Owain said with conviction.

Owain and Glyn went on to other subjects.

Glyn suggested to his friend that in his capacity as chief inspector, Wallon should bring in more recognized specialists in the fields of anthropology and archeology. Edward Grant and Brian Holmes are the colleagues that he mentioned before would be the best. The reason he gave was his concern about the ancient history of the cave.

"The floor of the cave needs to be investigated. Through the centuries sediment has been accumulating in layers on the floor. The cave sides have markings on them that need further interpretation. Up by the opening leading to the rock ledge, soot has accumulated, and there are other signs of smoke. This leads me to believe that there had been centuries of fire and smoke; perhaps we can discover long periods of ancient human habitation. The tunnels are another area which needs thorough researching. If Ted Sutter was planting evidence of gold, later to make a claim to a sizable vain of gold with shares to be sold to investors, you need to check on this possibility," Glyn told Owain.

Later, Owain was lying on Glyn's extra bed, puzzling over all the possible ways this case could turn. How much of the investigation included a criminal case, and how much was turning into an archeology dig? What would Superintendent Gordon want him to do? Sleep soon took over the tired mind of Chief Inspector Wallon, but not before he reviewed the nagging thoughts which Glyn had raised about his father's family. Why had Glyn made those remarks about his appearance? As sleep ended his thoughts, he dreamed of the vales and hills with the mist settling on them, and drifted off.

Shedweld's Business Dealings

In the morning, Owain awakened with a plan. He would have Glyn contact reputable specialists he knew in the fields of archeology and anthropology, hopefully connected, as Glyn was, to the university. They would be responsible for investigating the cave without arousing the attention of the press, and also encouraging the friendship and support of the environment groups.

Next, he wanted Sgts. McDowell and Jones to push forward the investigation of the murder and all possible connection to Shedweld, the businessman from Liverpool. If his business involved funding mining investments, there could be more to this case than they had uncovered at this point.

Just as he and Glyn had finished their coffee, Sgt. McDowell arrived with the car to take his boss back to headquarters. Glyn offered a cup to McDowell, who gladly accepted. Owain and Glyn discussed Owain's plans for the investigation of the cave using a new team of specialists.

On the way back to police headquarters, McDowell brought Wallon up to date on his and Jones's investigation into the murder. The fishermen who spotted the body in the bay were the same fishermen who watched the coffins being pushed overboard previously. The fishermen could not identify the body as that of one of the guys who had pushed the coffins into the water the other night. The boat the men had been in that night was too far out from shore for the fishermen to make a definite identification of this body. The coroners in the morgue were attempting to make a positive ID of the body in their report.

As far as locating Bill Denton and John Older, there was not very much to report. The investigation had raised the possibility that the men may have left the country. Tom Sutter had not been located. Glyn was going to try and locate Sutter through the university system.

Sgt. McDowell went on to explain to Chief Inspector Wallon that the gossip going around police headquarters in London was about Inspector Duvrey's mother. 'Queen Victoria,' as the boys like to refer to her, has been verbally striking out against Scotland Yard's special unit. She has even spoken to members of the royal family. Fortunately, she has not taken her case to the press. She claims that her son was unfairly and insultingly treated. The post that they gave him in the foreign office was a ruse to get him out of the country while the police tried to cover up a serious scandal concerning the theft of gold from the royal family's mine holdings in Wales.

"You can imagine, sir, what an uproar this has caused. The House of Lords has been gasping and sputtering all over their chambers. Thank goodness you aren't there, sir," said Sgt. McDowell.

"Yes, you are right, sergeant. Can't his mother understand that her son's conduct was very wrong to have involved the press in the investigation of such a serious case? The poor woman must be out of her mind. I know that she is very, very fond of her son, which must have blinded her to what he did. Lord Whitecoft and Sir Gordon did their very best to find another spot for him. Well, we can't waste our time on this problem. It is up to Sir Gordon to sort it out."

The North Wales headquarters was abuzz when they walked in. Owain went directly to Cadwell's office and walked right in. Cadwell was behind his desk and looked up as Owain entered. He motioned Owain to take a seat and offered him a cup of coffee.

"After hearing all the gossip from London, I would offer you something stronger, but it is business hours. Well, I guess you know that we are still on board to help you with this case if you want us to," Cadwell said.

"Definitely, I want you to stay involved. The murder is in your district; therefore we need to attack this together. Sgt. McDowell and I have gone over the murder, and would like to push the investigation. First, I have been speaking with a professor of geology named Anderson and he is willing to bring two more professors to help him investigate the cave. That way, we won't need to consider the study of the cave as a police problem. Professor Anderson and his two associates will be delicately handling the problems that might arise from the environmentalists. Hopefully, we can keep the press at bay. I will inform Sir Gordon of all the details, including proper certification of the men involved. You and your district, plus Sergeant McDowell and I can concentrate on the crimes.

"Now, we come to something that has been bothering me about this case. This wealthy businessman, Dirk Otis Shedweld, how much do we know about his business connections and the people he employs?"

Edwin Cadwell pushed his chair back from his desk and thought for a minute. "Shedweld has gained much respectability in the business and civic community during the ten years that he has been in this country. He is a citizen of Australia, and has offices both there and in Liverpool. He is very sharp with his business interests. From what we have gathered, he has residences in both places, plus this large cottage in the village of Dewi Sant. His wife stays in Australia, but I think he hoped that she would like the cottage and spend time in England. His business dealings center on his mining business, which has locations around the world. His salvage and scrap-metal business is very active here and in Liverpool, and his interest in a search for rare metals by his geological firm is very successful. When he built his cottage, he used a local contractor, Sam Conrad, and was given architectural plans from a friend of his. We have approached the contractor, and he is giving us a list of the workmen who were involved."

Owain sat intently listening to all that Edwin Cadwell had to say. He realized that in police work, speculation without proper evidence was not acceptable. Both he, as a chief inspector for a special branch of Scotland Yard, and Superintendent Cadwell, had to be very careful. From the way Cadwell had presented the information about this prominent international businessman, they would have to be cautious in their investigation. And they must not irritate him. Obviously, Shedweld had established political and financial contacts in England and other countries, especially Australia. "It's ironic," Owain thought, "that Duvrey had been sent to Australia at this time—and Ted Sutter was known to Duvrey, who brought him along to the cave; and Ted worked for Shedweld. Is there a connection?" Owain made note to locate Sutter, who was missing.

"Thank you," Owain said, "for informing me about what your people have discovered, and also cautioning me about this man, Shedweld. After what happened with Duvrey, I would not like to see another hassle arise again. I'm on my way with McDowell over to the morgue. Did you want to join us?"

"Yes, that is a good idea; I want to stay up to date on this case also."

The morgue had a dismal environment at best. The day outside was dreary as the four men entered. The pathologist and his lab assistant had the body ready for inspection.

According to their examination, the workman was strangled first, and then thrown over the side of a boat. The body showed no sign of injury from a struggle. The victim had been drinking; there was evidence of alcohol in his system. From this observation, it was suspected that the victim knew his assailant and perhaps had been drinking with him. The murderer was trying to make it appear as an accidental drowning. There was nothing out of the ordinary about the victim's clothing. He had been identified as an ex-convict who had served his time for armed robbery. Fingerprints had been taken to confirm the body's identification. Since the victim's records showed no known family, the contractor's office, when reached, volunteered to take care of the burial of their previous employee. Cadwell spoke up and suggested that the body be released to them unless Chief Inspector Wallon wanted it held.

Copies of the pathologist's reports would be given to Sgt. McDowell. Wallon agreed to the release of the body.

With that recorded, they returned to their cars and drove off. Cadwell and Jones returned to the police headquarters in North Wales. Owain had decided since it was close to the weekend that he would have Sgt. McDowell drive him down to the Ormes Victoria Hotel. Tom and Gwyneth had asked him to stay at their cottage.

After retrieving Owain's suitcases from his rooms at the hotel where they were staying, McDowell drove Owain over to the Lewis's cottage behind the Ormes Victoria. Gwyneth came out to greet them and invited Sgt. McDowell to come in for a cup of tea. Owain begged off and left Gwyneth and his sergeant to enjoy their refreshments, while he took a stroll down to the little beach across from the hotel. He hoped the waters of the bay would calm his headache.

Meanwhile, McDowell said to Gwyneth, "I am worried about the chief inspector. He needs more time off. Maybe a couple of days with his friends will help. After his accident, I don't think he had enough time, in my opinion, to recover from that blow to the head from the car accident."

"Don't worry, sergeant, we will see that he rests."

Down by the water's edge, Owain stared out at the bay and at the fishing boats bobbing on the water. A short distance away on the beach stood a young woman; but she did not appear to notice him. Her slim figure seemed almost frail. Her long blond hair fell loose around her shoulders. The jacket she was wearing would not be enough to keep her dry from the light drizzle that was falling. He thought of walking over to her and offering his coat, when a young man approached with an umbrella and guided her back towards the hotel. As they passed him, Owain could not help noticing how fragile and lovely she appeared.

The young couple disappeared into the hotel. Owain decided that he best return to Tom's cottage. Still, he could not help standing there for a while, gazing out to sea. His mind lately seemed to be playing tricks on him. He kept imagining that he was not alone. It was not a worrisome feeling, but rather a reassuring one. When he turned to see who else might be around, he saw no one. Shaking off this momentary distraction, he headed back up to the hotel. Tom was standing in the doorway of the hotel, and gave his old friend a bear-hug greeting.

"Owain, you look terrible. Come on in. I will draw you a nice pint and we can sit down and talk. Sergeant McDowell has just left. Have you had anything to eat since breakfast?" asked Tom.

"No, we grabbed my suitcase and left for here. I am so glad to see you, old friend. This case is testing my reserve energy. So, they can do without me for the weekend. I know. You need not tell me that my aunt is probably worried. She is like a mother to me since I lost mine."

"Listen, don't be concerned. Gwyneth has called her, and explained that you are staying with us, and that eased her mind," said Tom.

"Say, who is that lovely young woman who just walked in with a young man, just ahead of me?" asked Owain.

"Isn't she beautiful? The man with her is her brother and another brother is also here with her. They came in yesterday. Their last name is Montgomery. Evidently, she has suffered some sort of emotional shock. What, I don't know. The brothers are always close by her side. A doctor from London has been here to see her. They keep very much to themselves to the point that they insist on eating in one of the side dining rooms. No one makes any attempt to speak to them, except the staff. They are staying on the top floor in the only suite in the hotel. I have the feeling that they are waiting for someone to join them—an extra bedroom has been reserved next to the suite," said Tom.

"Montgomery is an old family name from the north of England. Did they give you an address?"

"Only the telephone number of their solicitor in London, who made the reservations. The law firm is known for handling the affairs of titled families,"commented Tom. "I checked."

"Really!" said Owain. "I wonder who they are. I must confess, this clientele of yours, Tom, is very well connected."

"Look, Owain, one of my waiters has brought you a plate of smoked herring, crisps, and a salad."

"My, Tom, thanks—this looks delicious."

"You can thank Gwyneth, she has improved our menu; and we are drawing a very upscale clientele. She has also taken over the redecorating of the main rooms downstairs as well as the bedrooms. The owners of this hotel are very pleased, and it has saved them a lot of money in designing and decorating fees. Since we met while you and I were on that case in Shropshire, I wasn't aware until after we were married that she had a degree in interior design and her license in Michigan. When you finish your meal, I will take you back to the cottage, and then you can relax before dinner this evening."

After putting away his clothes in the cottage guest room, Owain had to admit that he and Glyn stayed up very late the night before. Looking out the window, Owain could see down past the hotel to the bay below. The mist was drifting in, the fishing boats had come in to dock, and the view looked so peaceful. As he gazed down to the spot where he had seen the young woman before, he could swear that he could see her there again. What the devil would bring her out in the rain? I hope she is not suicidal. While he watched, two young men ran up to her with a rain coat, and brought her back up to the hotel.

After a wonderful dinner at the cottage, Gwyneth, Tom, and Owain sat around their cozy fireplace with the last of the wine and snifters of brandy. They spent most of the time catching up on all that had been happening at the hotel, up at Gorwyn Hall, and back in Michigan, where Gwyneth's family lived. Her brother was doing well in law school, and her parents were planning to make a trip to Wales soon. Owain's eyelids started to droop, and Tom suggested that he had to return to the hotel for the late-night check. Gwyneth planned to go with him. Owain said goodnight and went upstairs.

Again Owain wandered over to the window. The weather had cleared, and there was a full moon. An enjoyable scene—until he noticed that the young woman was out there again. This time her brothers were with her, and she had on a warm coat and scarf. Oh, well, he thought—this did not concern him. He turned off the light and went to sleep. He was to dream about many things, but in his dreams that lovely young woman was there. She appeared so unhappy and weary.

In the morning, he chuckled to himself. Owain, you are fascinated by her. However, she looks like she might not be very approachable. He went to the hotel dining room for breakfast. Both Tom and Gwyneth were occupied with the business of managing the hotel. He took his cup of coffee out onto the veranda, and was relaxing there when he realized that someone had come up behind him—the beautiful young creature that had been in his dreams was now standing next to him.

"Good Morning," smiled Owain.

"Good Morning," she replied "I noticed you yesterday on the beach. You gave me the impression that you were perhaps—how, can I say it?" She struggled to find the right words. "Lost in thought." she commented.

"I am recovering from a head injury that I received in a car accident recently, and my mind is seeking some quiet time and re-laxation for a few days. Now! Why am I telling you this . . .?" Owain paused with some temporary embarrassment. Then he continued again. "I feel fine, and I am glad to take the weekend off to spend time with my good friends, Tom and Gwyneth," Owain said having recovered from his recent embarrassment.

"You look so familiar. Have we met before? I'm Francesca Mont-gomery. I know that I must have seen you somewhere," she said.

Before Owain could respond, her brother approached them.

"Oh! James this is—I'm sorry; I have forgotten your name, sir."

Owain was embarrassed again, but introduced himself. "My name is Owain Wallon."

"My brother, James Montgomery," said Francesca.

"Yes, how do you do, my sister is correct; you do look very fa-miliar. Have we met before?" said James Montgomery. "Perhaps at a party. . . . or on the links?"

"I don't think so…. Sorry, I must go. It has been very nice to have met you both."

Owain hurriedly handed one of the waiters his coffee cup and left. "What has happened to me?" Owain thought as he walked out to the cottage. "I am acting like a silly school boy."

Gwyneth noticed Owain as he came in, and commented that he looked a little flushed. Owain shrugged his shoulders and mum-bled half to her, something about meeting the Montgomerys. Then continued his response to Gwyneth, he adds in a proper gentle-manly way "Fascinating people you know."

Gwyneth looked over at him and laughed, "Yes, they are," she said. "Oh, by the way, Tom told me that Lord Peter Whitecoft and his daughter, Joanna, are coming over for dinner tonight. I don't believe you have ever met Joanna. She is quite attractive and not as timid as Francesca. You have been invited by Lord Peter Whitecoft to join them. I will be there also, but Tom won't. He has his duties at the hotel, and plans to join us after dinner. It seems that Lord

Whitecoft, the Montgomery brothers—James, and Sir Harold—, plus an important business man have things to discuss after dinner. I have invited Joanna Whitecoft, Francesca Montgomery, and you to come over to the cottage for after-dinner drinks and coffee. Does that plan suit you?"

"Absolutely," responded Owain. "What is the attire?"

"Sports jacket and tie. Do you need to borrow from Tom?"

"No, I'm fine," responded Owain. As he left for his room upstairs, Owain reviewed in his mind. Who was the business man coming for a meeting at the hotel but not to dinner? He must speak with Tom about this meeting.

That evening they all congregated in the private dining room. The ladies were attired in soft chiffon and silk dresses. Owain could not help admiring how beautiful they looked. His conservative tweed Jacket and tie was fine for the occasion, he thought. The other men came over from the bar, similarly dressed. Gwyneth had arranged the seating. Lord Peter was at one end of the table and Sir Harold Montgomery, Francesca's older brother, was at the other. Joanna Whitecoft was on her father's right. She was a stunning young woman. She obviously wished to be included in the conversation at Owain's end of the table. Francesca was on Sir Harold's right; Owain was on his left, and Gwyneth was on Lord Peter's left.

James had gone to meet the "important businessman" for the meeting afterwards. Sir Harold spent most of the dinner time conversing with Owain, and across the table Francesca gazed at Owain admiringly. Lord Peter and his two dinner companions chatted on while Joanna listened in on the conversation at Owain's end of the table. Owain felt somewhat uncomfortable with the attention on him. The others at his end of the table didn't appear to notice. He tried to steer the conversation onto lighter topics, but Sir Harold was most interested to hear about Owain and his position as chief inspector under Sir William Gordon, who was a friend of his as well as Lord Whitecoft.

"My goodness, Owain, you do look very familiar. Sir Gordon tells me that you have outstanding abilities, and that your talents may be wasted in a police career. Lord Peter commented favorably about you to us also," said Sir Harold.

Again Owain felt uncomfortable about his resemblance to someone to which they all referred. This had been brought up this morning by the Montgomerys. When had Sir Harold had time to talk with Sir Gordon about him? What was behind their comments, he wondered. They had the best of him that was for sure, because he did not have the slightest idea who it was, and this would continue to bother him.

After dinner, Owain escorted the three ladies over to Gwyneth's cottage. As they were passing the lobby entrance, Owain spotted James returning with the wealthy businessman. At once, Tom, who was behind the front desk, realized the man in the expensive business suit was none other than Dirk Otis Shedweld. He stepped over to Owain and whispered in his ear: "That is Shedweld." The two men were hurrying into the meeting room, and Owain was sure that Shedweld had not spotted Tom pointing him out. Why hadn't Dirk Otis Shedweld joined them for dinner?

Back in the sitting room of the Lewis's cottage, Owain poured glasses of sherry and brandy from an elegant set of crystal decanters. Gwyneth was a great hostess, and the young women were chatting away about the dinner and how good the food and service had been. Owain contentedly sat with his snifter of brandy. As he observed Joanna Whitecoft, he noticed again that she was a strikingly good-looking athletic young woman. Gwyneth had told him that Joanna was very active in the local environmentalist group in Snowdonia, and enjoyed hiking.

Sitting opposite Joanna was Francesca, the lovely creature who had caught his attention at the beach and then again at dinner tonight. She appeared less sad and more relaxed this evening than she had been yesterday down on the beach. At the peak of her abilities as a hostess, Gwyneth was glowing and having a wonderful time. Tom entered and joined them. He had seen to the staff and decided to come join the group at the cottage. Owain and he talked about the years that they had known Glyn Anderson, who had always been interested in geology and sports. Since Tom and Gwyneth had moved to the cottage they had seen Glyn once or twice while attending meetings of the local environmentalist group. Joanna Whitecoft was also a member of this group. Dirk

Otis Shedweld was known to frequent the hotel dining room from to time.

Owain thought to himself, so that is Shedweld. He was a confident looking man in his fifties, but then swindlers generally are. They want to convey the look of someone who can be trusted.

VI

Murder on the Hiking Trail

Sitting around the breakfast table the next morning at the hotel, Owain and Tom conversed about the previous evening.

"Tom, I am a little confused by these people who keep referring to the fact that I resemble someone they have met before. Even Glyn Anderson mentioned something about it. He inquired into my father's background," commented Owain with some irritation in his voice.

"Come on, Owain, I wouldn't be concerned. People are always noticing someone who they may or may not have met before. You are a good-looking guy, so take it as a compliment. The girls at university were all chasing after you. However, you pretty much ignored them. You were very serious, and your studies came first. Girls love to flirt with the strong, silent type and you certainly were that. Have your aunt and uncle talked about your resemblance to someone in the family perhaps?

"I have not mentioned anything to them recently; and I am not comfortable about making inquiries. Because when I was younger, I sought out information about my parents. Evidently, my mother was very attractive, and everyone adored her. As for my father well, he is just mentioned as one of the Wallons. I guess they blamed him for the car accident that killed both of them. There are no photographs around that I have seen. Aunt Catherine becomes teary-eyed when her sister Elizabeth's name is mentioned."

A waitress interrupted them to announce that Sergeant Mc-Dowell was on the phone and asked for Chief Inspector Wallon. Tom looked over at him with some concern. This was supposed to be time off for his friend to relax.

"Well, so much for rest and relaxation," said Owain as he returned to his chair to take the phone call.

"McDowell, what news do you have for me?" asked Owain.

"Ted Sutter has been murdered. His body was found on the hiking trail not very far from the cave entrance. A group of hikers who found him went for help. . . . Sir, are you there?" asked McDowell as he waited for his boss's response.

"Yes, I am here," responded Owain as he considered this new turn in the case. "I need you to come over to the hotel right away. We must start investigating this second murder immediately. Have you interviewed the hikers? How was Sutter killed? Where is his body now?"

"I will leave right away and bring you up to date as we go over to the morgue, sir."

He and McDowell had the difficult position in this case of working with a regional superintendent and his police staff. Scotland Yard special branch agents are to assist only in the investigation. Owain was very aware that the police station was understaffed and they needed his help. Budgets had been cut and the assistance of McDowell and him had been well receive and needed. Inspector Duvrey had come in and insulted the local authorities. Superintendent Cadwell of this district appeared to be carefull about investigating Shedwell and his business. There have been two murders, graving robbing and the dumping of evidence in the bay.

Chief Inspector Wallon's professional mind once again went into gear. "With this new perplexing development, there is more information we must have about those coffins in the bay, McDowell. Sutter was the last person seen with the rock samples. Those samples might be in one of those coffins."

Cadwell didn't seem interested in retrieving the coffins because of the cost. It would require special equipment and divers. Everyone assumed that they were chucked into the bay empty to get rid of them. It occurred to me, sir, that if coffins where empty, why did they sink to the bottom so rapidly?" replied McDowell.

Owain frowned. "Well, I am interested. See to the permits, and hire divers to go into the bay tomorrow. Tell Cadwell that I have requested that the two coffins be brought to the surface but not opened until they are taken to the lab, where you and I can be present. I presume District Police Headquarters has facilities to do investigation work on the coffins. If not, let me know. We will make other arrangements. It has occurred to me that these coffins were not just disposed of empty. Retrieve them before someone else decides to salvage them.

"By the way, last night Dirk Otis Shedweld was here at the hotel meeting with Lord Peter Whitecoft and Sir Harold Montgomery. He did not see me, and I made no attempt to speak with him. For some reason, I have noticed, Superintendent Cadwell is unusually careful about making any attempt to investigate this man Shedweld. And in fact he has suggested that Shedweld has many friends in important places and that he would not like to embarrass the man. What do you think about that, McDowell?"

"I don't know sir but, it bears conducting further investigation by the Special Branch into Mr. Shedweld's background and business affairs, I would suggest."

"Yes, you are correct; I will contact Sir Gordon tomorrow first thing. Today, we need to conduct a full scale investigation into Sutter's murder." The chief inspector was taking charge of this case. The local police headquarters seemed to be avoiding opening an investigation which might include Shedweld.

Owain approached Tom with a favor: Since he was lacking in a business wardrobe down here at the shore, would Tom be able to lend him a dark suit?

"Of course I will," said Tom, and reached for the phone to call Gwyneth to have one of his suits ready for Owain to try on.

"Thanks, Tom."

"What's happened? Do you have to go over to police headquarters today? It is Sunday; can't this wait until tomorrow?"

"Ted Sutter, the geologist who worked for Dirk Otis Shedweld's geology firm and who was selected by Duvrey for his investigation of the cave, has been murdered," explained Owain.

McDowell arrived and Owain left with him. He told Tom that he would keep in touch and asked him to explain to Gwyneth that she should not mention any of this business to his aunt. Tom agreed—and realized this case was taking on new turns every day.

Arriving at Cadwell's office, they went over the report that the hikers made concerning the discovery of the body. Cadwell explained what he knew as they read the report.

The ground had been seriously trampled down by the hikers—unfortunately. There was very little evidence to collect. Ted Sutter had apparently been struck from behind with a heavy rod of some sort, perhaps a hiking stick. He had his wallet with money and ID in his hiking bag. He was dressed in regular hiking clothes. The blow to Sutter's head had to be made by someone who was very strong. There wasn't a hiking stick in evidence. Cadwell said that Mr. Shedweld had been brought in to identify the body. At that time he showed mild shock and concern over what had happened. He said that since Ted Sutter had no relatives in this country, he would see that the body was returned to Sydney for burial—and another connection to Sydney was noted in the case. The pathologist had determined the time of death and would put it in his full report after conducting the autopsy; the report would be available Monday morning.

Owain, McDowell, and Cadwell sat in his office discussing motive and possible suspects. Was this murder connected to the other one from the bay? If so it would be very important for those coffins to be retrieved in the morning and brought back to the police labs for investigation. These deaths may be involved with the contents of those coffins. By now, Owain was convinced that they were. Sutter had been one of Duvrey's team who collected objects for the bags that were put into the car when they left the cave crime site.

Owain and McDowell left for The Ormes Victoria Hotel, since they would be needed at the bay early. Tom Lewis was glad to give McDowell a hotel room for the night.

Before anyone realized what was happening, McDowell had the coffins located and raised from the bay bottom. As the truck carted the coffins away from the pier, McDowell drove up to the hotel for Owain. During the drive back to the lab, Owain explained his plan to keep all information about the investigation into the coffins secure, and not to have the press informed until they had the opportunity of examining the contents of the coffins. He had informed Sir Gordon in London concerning these latest developments and the murder of Sutter. He requested more detailed information on Shedwell's business records and Sutter's Australian records.

Superintendent Cadwell, Detective Jones, and Chief Inspector Wallon viewed the body of Ted Sutter at the morgue. They studied the deep wounds made to the back and front of Sutter's head by a heavy instrument. It appeared to have been a very violent attack. There were no other marks on the body to verify that there had been a fight or struggle before the deadly blows were struck. After receiving a full report, they left for the special lab examining room set up to receive the coffins.

Two lab technicians as well as a forensic man were standing by. The coffins were placed on two separate tables. After a brief examination of the outsides, Owain ordered that they be opened carefully one at a time. A crime photographer was there; ready to take pictures of the contents.

The first coffin was pried open, and the top set to the side. With large lamps switched on, the group peered inside the coffin. Cadwell exclaimed, "Rocks—they must have been put on the bottom to weigh down the box."

Owain told the photographer to take pictures of the contents, and then the technicians could remove the rocks and place them on a separate table. More pictures were to be taken of each rock. He wanted Glyn Anderson to examine them later. An exact count of the rocks must be logged in to the records and labeled. Then the rocks can be stored in a box. Supt. Cadwell looked astonished but said nothing. Detective Jones looked mystified. They wondered what was so special about these rocks and why were they being photographed separately.

The technicians moved to the second coffin and proceeded to open the lid as before. They suspected that a body might be inside. However, when they looked into the interior of the second coffin, they were very surprised to see large and small bags. Again, Owain ordered the photographer to take photographs first, before any of the bags were removed for examination.

Then one bag was removed to another table. It was made of water proof material. Gently, the bag was unsealed, and the contents removed.

"Bones," said Detective Jones. "Those are probably the bones that we watched being wrapped in blankets and removed from the cave when Inspector Duvrey brought his team to investigate the bodies on the cave floor. Later, the corpses had been identified as the bodies of two people from the village of Dewi Sant."

The next bag was brought over to a table and unsealed. Large items of Celtic jewelry and parts of old armour were removed from the bag. These items had dirt and other materials attached to the metal pieces. Two small but heavy bags were added to the collection on the second table. After again unsealing them, gold coins of various kinds were found inside. The group stood looking at the collection with amazement.

Chief Inspector Wallon ordered that a full inventory and cataloguing of each bag must be made with pictures of all items taken. "No object must be removed from this room, and tight security must be maintained," he declared. "All the contents of this room will be part of a criminal investigation. No statement or word can be announced or given out to the press until I have brought in my own team of investigators to examine these objects. It will be necessary to find out if these objects have been stolen. If not, where were the objects found?"

After he had time to collect himself, Caldwell agreed and assured that his department could be trusted to keep this unusual find confidential. Most of the group of technicians, after standing in shocked amazement, got down to work. Going from the expectation of dead bodies to the realization of a large and valuable treasure in their lab had grabbed the attention of everyone. Sgt. McDowell was to stay in the lab until the room was sealed for the night and then he could return to his hotel near the police station.

Owain and Cadwell met in a room down the hall to talk.

"As I suspected," said Owain, "these coffins had a purpose which we did not recognize at first. When the bodies were discarded in the cave, it was to use these coffins to hold the treasure, and then to rebury it in the church yard. The rocks and the bones were added by Duvrey's crew to the second coffin when they realized that these coffins were about to be dug up once more, they knew that the authorities would find the treasure taken from the cave. They had to retrieve the coffins with the treasures, and hide them someplace else. Obviously, underwater, and in sealed bags, these items would be safe from discovery. The man who was killed down by the bay must have observed them, and was perhaps blackmailing the group. The gang could not let him live.

"We do not have any answers for the killing of the geologist Ted Sutter, or the location of John Older and Bill Denton, the two who were with him that day at the cave. Where are these men? How much is the contractor, Sam Conrad, who built the cottage, involved? We need more answers. I am afraid that we must question Dirk Otis Shedweld," stated Chief Inspector Wallon.

Cadwell was decidedly uncomfortable with this idea, and Owain took note of the superintendent's reluctance to involve Shedweld or to talk with him. Again Cadwell tried to explain that Shedweld was a much-respected member of the community.

Owain replied, went on to say, "Respected member of the community or not, his cottage and land were very much involved with part of this crime." Cadwell had to agree.

Owain was driven back to the hotel by Detective Jones. He entered the lobby and was immediately approached by Tom, who commented on how smart Owain looked in his suit. Owain laughed and said that he was very grateful to have such a good friend. He took Tom aside to confide in his old partner from Scotland Yard.

"This case has two murders. One person, Ted Sutter the geologist, was directly tied to Shedweld and employed in his geology business, and was a citizen of Australia. The other murder was of an employee who worked for the construction manager for Shedweld's cottage. Then there are two missing persons who were on Duvrey's team that he brought in to investigate the cave while I was recovering from the car accident. They were friends of Tom Sutter, who was just murdered. Their names are Denton and Older. One was an anthropologist and the other an archeologist. We can't find a trace of these two, and we need both these men who we need brought in for questioning. Sergeant McDowell is going over to Shedweld's geology firm and also his mining company and salvage business, located in Liverpool. Also, we need to question the contractor of Shedweld's cottage."

"Do you think it is possible that Duvrey is involved in this business?" asked Tom.

"I don't know. He is in Sydney, Australia. Shedweld's firm has offices there," Owain added.

"Oh, by the way," said Tom. "Gwyneth is thinking about making a trip to her family's home and she has invited James and Francesca to come with her. She thinks her mother would love to entertain the Mongomerys. Her friends would be enthusiastic about giving parties for them as well. It might be a change of pace for Francesca. She has never been to the United States before. I would stay and manage the hotel, of course, and you would be welcome to share the cottage with me whenever you need a place to stay near District Headquarters."

"Thanks, Tom. Unless new developments come in soon, I will be returning to my office and my own place in London. But what's up for dinner? Is Gwyneth making any plans?"

"Oh! Yes, you know she is. James and Francesca and Joanna are coming for a casual dinner in the restaurant. Sir Harold has left for London; and Lord Peter has gone back to his country estate. Both Gwyneth and I are going to be busy tonight with a catered party in the private dining room. So have fun. Dinner is at seven and they plan to get together for drinks in the lounge at six. Until then you are a free man," laughed Tom.

"Paperwork—I do have paper that I must attend to before dinner," said Owain.

As the grand old clock in the lobby chimed six, the group gathered in the lounge for drinks. Owain was again relaxing in his tweed sports jacket, and James was wearing his yacht club navy blazer. The girls came in laughing in tailored silk dresses. Gwyneth joined them for a minute to say hello and to apologize for not being free to join them. She suggested that Francesca tell them about the plans to travel with her to America.

"What's this?—you are taking off for America. It will do you good, both of you," said Joanna. "I am deep in a project for our environmentalist club here in Snowdonia. We want these greedy gold-seeking robbers to stop destroying our beautiful hills with their earth-moving equipment."

"I thought they used pans to collect the gold from stream beds," remarked Francesca.

"Oh no, they want to go after the gold under the ground."

"But, Joanna, how much gold is left in Wales? They have been mining gold since the time of Julius Caesar. Isn't it pretty well mined out?" asked Francesca.

"Oh! According to what my father has been told, this area of Wales has not seen the last of gold ore finds. It will take heavy earth-moving equipment to reach the veins of gold. We plan to stop them from tearing up any more hillsides to replenish their greed." Joanna said this firmly, with a very stern look on her face.

"Who told your father, Lord Peter, that there was proof of gold veins here in Wales?" asked Owain.

"Why, this businessman from Liverpool. Let me see if I can remember his name…. Oh yes, Shedweld. Strange name, don't you think?" responded Joanna as she gave Owain a warm smile.

James Montgomery chimed in: "Yes, that is the name. My bother Harold talked about him. Shedweld and his geological firm have had success in locating places to start their excavations."

Joanne repeated firmly, "Well, they won't! We will stop them. I have to speak with my father again about these plans. He assured me that the site was in Australia, not Wales."

Owain sat quietly listening to the conversation. Sir Harold and Lord Peter Whitecoft were definitely involved in one of Shedweld's financial schemes. He was not happy to hear this information and remembered their meeting at the hotel with Shedweld.

The waiter announced that their table was ready for them in the dining room. Owain went over to speak with McDowell, who was enjoying his dinner in the bar. They had spent the rest of the late afternoon there working on reports. Owain informed him what he had heard concerning Shedweld's business contacts with Sir Harold and Lord Peter. McDowell took out his notebook and entered this new information concerning Shedweld and his business deals.

VII

Joanna Sets Her Sights on Owain

Owain awoke the next morning after his first sound sleep in a long time. He, Joanna, Francesca, and James had had a great evening joking and telling silly stories from their school days. Francesca was improving more and more every day. She didn't need to wander down to the shoreline and cause everyone to be concerned for her safety. James was able to relax more, and not have to be responsible for every move that Francesca made. Joanna was a delightful conversationalist. The story that she told about her friends joking around at school gave Owain the idea that she had been a bit of a handful for her nannies and schoolteachers. She was likable and bright, as well as good-looking, and she had a very confident outlook on life as well. Gwyneth was downstairs fixing coffee. So, he had better get dressed and pack up his things.

Owain had decided to return to the London offices today.

After returning Tom's suit, and offering to pay for the dry cleaning, he headed down to Tom's office in the hotel. Tom was waiting for him, and they were off to the dining room for breakfast with Sgt. McDowell. There was the issue of securing the objects found in the coffins, and driving over to the cave for a look around before McDowell took him to the afternoon train for London. Owain wanted to make sure that Glyn and his team, Edward Grant and Brian Holmes had the information that they needed.

After the shock of what had been found in the coffins yesterday, Cadwell today was coping with new information. He maintained that he could secure the objects at his district headquarters for the time being; they would be safe in a locked security room to which he held the only key. McDowell visited Mr. Shedweld, who politely cooperated with noncommittal responses to McDowell's questions that supplied very little information. Wallon and Cadwell accepted McDowell's suggestion to speak with Shedweld's cleaning woman, and some of the people in town.

All that McDowell was able to discover was that Shedweld had had several visitors, and some had stayed the night. The cleaning woman told him that there were at least three beds to change each week. She had never seen his visitors; they were gone when she arrived to clean. She also did the shopping for Shedweld, and he went through a lot of food. The cleaning woman complained about the amount of clothes she had had to wash.

McDowell reported to his boss that he had visited the geology firm of Shedweld's. Again, the two men in the office did not have very much to say. They of course knew Ted Sutter, and had a few comments to make about him. As for the other two men, Denton and Older, they didn't know who they were. McDowell closed his verbal report by saying he thought most of the people he had interviewed were holding back information. Without having cause to charge them, he didn't see how he could bring them into the station for further questioning. He tried to get in to see Sam Conrad, the construction manager for the cottage, but he was out of town. Everyone had been courteous but had given him very little helpful information.

Owain planned to make another visit to the cave site. Glyn Anderson should be out there with the other specialists. So Owain and McDowell carried out a stack of reports and folders of photographs to the government Land Rover. They would go over to the cave, and then on to the train station. Cadwell promised that he would have Jones continue to dig for more information; and he would report to Chief Inspector Wallon in London as soon as something developed.

McDowell was downcast about the lack of information. Owain instructed him to send reports to Sir Gordon concerning Shedweld's reluctance to give out very much information. As they drove over to the cave, Owain tried to cheer up his sergeant, who prided himself on his interviewing ability. Also, McDowell needed to report to Chief Supt. Gordon the discovery of the items in the coffins. He told McDowell that he would put more pressure on the London department to investigate Shedweld's business ventures. Joanna had said that her father was told the gold mine which he was invested in was located in Australia. They needed to contact the Australian government about the gold mine licenses that were given to Shedweld. If the investors and Lord Whitecoft were being taken advantage of financially, then he had to be made to stop any illegal use of investors' funds. Also, as a part of this investigation without alerting anyone, there must be a way to find out who was staying at Shedweld's house.

"McDowell, see if you can set up a surveillance team to watch the cottage. Hopefully, Superintendent Cadwell will be cooperative about sending some of his people to help with the surveillance. Let me know what success you have."

As they approached the archeology dig team at the cave, Owain could see Glyn standing outside along with two other men.

"Hello, Owain, glad you could come by. We have made some startling discoveries. Let me introduce you to Dr. Edward Grant and Dr. Brian Holmes. Edward is an anthropologist, and Brian is an archeologist. Both are very much respected in their fields of expertise. They have taken time off from their other projects to help us out here."

Chief Inspector Wallon stepped forward and introduced himself and Sgt. McDowell. He told them that he was headed back to London for a few days and that Sergeant McDowell would remain on the scene in his absence.

"Now, what have you discovered?"

They entered the cave to find very carefully laid-out grid lines for the dig. On the side, they had placed several objects on a table as well as pieces of wood samples for carbon dating, and small stone carvings.

Glyn began, "From what we have found so far, this was a burial site for an important member of a tribe. We will have to wait for exact carbon dates, but it looks like this burial could have occurred during Roman times or earlier. The site has been disturbed, probably by grave robbers, and pieces have been removed. The floor had been replaced and raked. The plan was probably to return for more relics later. There is a lot of work to be done here, and we will have to find some way to keep out the curious onlookers especially should the robbers return."

Owain was anxious to tell Glyn, Edward, and Brian what had been discovered when the coffins were retrieved from the bay and opened at police headquarters. He had brought in the files and photos, and handed them over for Glyn and the others to study.

"Good heavens, look at these pictures!" the team members said. "You found these bags in the coffins in the bay which you think were stored here?"

"Let us review what we know about this case. When the men dug up the last two coffins at the Shedweld's construction site, they brought them here to the cave, and dumped out the two bodies that had been inside. Then the old metal objects and gold coins that they had dug up were packed in watertight bags and loaded into the coffins. They buried the newly filled coffins in the grave-yard back in the village of Dewi Sant. But when we planned to dig up these two grave sites to rebury the bodies that we had found in the cave, the robbers had to go back to the village graveyard to remove the original coffins, and add the bones and more rocks and skeleton bones that they had collected at the cave. During Inspector Duvrey's investigation of the cave with his team, the bodies were here, and the bones were also here. A policeman with them at the time realized Older had picked up a small shiny object next to one of the bodies. Denton found the skeletons, wrapped them in a blanket, and loaded them into his car. Sutter had collected rocks from the tunnel, and loaded them in bags that were taken out to his car. Before the coffins were dumped into the bay, these items were added to the contents of the coffins. The photographs that you are looking at, of the contents of those two coffins, are now se-curely stored at District Police Headquarters. Only Superintendent Cadwell has the key to the security room."

Glyn Anderson's team was very excited to take a look at these items. Owain explained that at this point the items were evidence in a police investigation of two murders. After the coffins were seen being dumped into the bay, the body of a workman was found nearby.

"The geologist, Ted Sutter, who had accompanied Inspector Duvrey to the cave during the first investigation, was murdered on the hiking trail not very far from this cave last Saturday." The group, including Glyn, was shocked. Owain decided not to tell them all the details since the investigation was ongoing.

Owain recommended that they continue their study of the cave and document everything they found, especially if it might pertain to the identity of the robbers. He would be returning soon, and would bring with him the papers that would authorize their study of the objects from the coffins which had been secured at police headquarters.

Reluctantly, they agreed but continued to speculate about the bones and the other objects. Glyn showed great interest in the pictures of the stones that were found in one of the coffins. He explained that he had been searching the tunnels, and concluded that the rocks came from this tunnel, or somewhere else to substantiate the possibility of gold. Owain and McDowell left the group deep in conversation, and drove off to find a place near the train station for some lunch.

At lunch, the men went over the evidence in the case again. Glyn had requested copies of the photos taken at the lab, and Owain authorized McDowell to give Glyn's team a set of photographs so that they could study them. Soon it was time for the train to pull out and Owain left McDowell with instructions in the hopes that more evidence would be found before he returned in a few days.

Sitting on the train, Owain caught up on the news from the papers and started a new novel he had purchased at a book store near the train station. The book that he had chosen was about the location of the Knights Templar chapel in Scotland. This topic was *always* of interest to him since during his last case he had been involved in locating a Welsh relic.

Upon arriving at his place, located off Sloan's Square, he found a phone message waiting for him from Joanna Whitecoft, who had also just returned to London and wanted him to join her for dinner. It was too late to meet with Sir Gordon today; he would have left his offices by this time. Owain enjoyed contemplating having dinner with Joanna that evening. After calling her and making arrangements for seven at a restaurant she had suggested, he sat down to concentrate on his reports.

Before he realized it, the time left for his work was over, and he needed to consider what attire would be best for the evening with Joanna. She had selected a very exclusive French bistro, not exactly in his budget range, but what the hell; it was about time for him to "live it up," so to speak. He decided on a suit which Gwyneth had talked him into buying when they had gone on a shopping trip together ages ago. At that time, he was on another case with Tom, who was still on the staff at the Yard.

In those days Owain could not have foreseen the future and what it held for Gwyneth and Tom. Now, they were happily married. She had been a beautiful bride; and Tom had been very handsome in his groom's attire. Owain had stood next to him as his best man. The wedding took place at the Lydley's elegant private club on a lake in Michigan. Guy, Gwyneth's brother, was also part of the wedding party. Tom's parents could not make the wedding, so Aunt Catherine and Uncle Hywel had represented Tom's side. After the wedding, the bride and groom returned to Wales.

All the wonderful memories of Tom and Gwyneth's wedding came flooding back to him, as he dressed for the dinner. Joanna had not been in the picture at that time. Gwyneth's father, William Lydley, knew Lord Peter Whitecoft, who gave a lovely silver service for a wedding gift. William and Lord Peter had been at Oxford together. Joanna and Gwyneth became friends when she and Tom returned to Wales. Joanna spent much of her time as secretary of the environmentalist group nearby.

Owain rushed out of his building and hailed a cab to pick up Joanna at her father's London townhouse. When he arrived, she was ready and waiting in the vestibule. She came out to meet him looking extraordinarily attractive in her slim red short-sleeved dress with her skirt swirling around her shapely legs. She briskly came down the steps. For warmth she wore a large black cashmere shawl, and she carried a black Chanel evening bag. Owain, who had stepped out of the cab to greet her, was overwhelmed, to say the least. With her high-heeled slim backless shoes, Joanna was almost as tall as he was. Her pretty, dark curly hair was cut short and spruced up with styling mouse. For jewelry she wore only small earrings and a bracelet that complimented her cosmopolitan look. Admiring her as she sat next to him in the cab, all that Owain could think to say was, "You look wonderful."

As they entered the restaurant, the maître d' came up to them immediately, addressing Joanna as 'her ladyship.' All eyes were on them as they were led to a table towards the back of the restaurant, located away from most other tables. Owain strained not to feel uncomfortable as the eyes of other patrons followed them. Once they were seated, the waiter approached Owain and asked if he wished to see the wine menu.

"They have an outstanding selection of wines," commented Joanna. "Yes, we would love to see the wine list, thank you, Andre."

With a careful sideward glance towards her, Owain showed an expression of some alarm. Joanna took his hand and squeezed it. "Father wants to do something nice for us this evening." Owain glanced her way again with an unsettled feeling. This evening was not starting out the way he had anticipated it would. Joanna in her take charge state of mind was pushing her plan too fast.

But the rest of the evening ran smoothly. Owain picked a very nice Chateauneuf de Pape that he remembered William Lydley, Gwyneth's father, talked about. They shared the specialty of the house, which included three delicious courses, followed by after-dinner drinks. During the cab ride back to Joanna's place she invited Owain up for brandy and coffee. Sitting in the Whitecoft's townhouse library, Owain asked if Lord Peter would mind if they lounged in her father's library. He thought of this as her father's personal place. Joanna thought of it as far more romantic than the formal drawing room a cross the hall.

"He is out of town, and the servants have the time off," she said. "I don't like all the old ways of always having servants constantly at your beck and call. Usually, when I am in town for a few days, I give them time off to go see their families." Owain relaxed, swirling his brandy. A quiet voice in his brain for just a moment gave out a warning. He was seriously attracted to this lovely woman. Joanna's hand strayed over to touch his hand; her unmistakable romantic charm dissolved his resistance.

Early in the morning, he returned to his place to change and go to his office at the Yard. Somehow the frustration of this case did not weigh him down as much as it had yesterday. Joanna and he had decided to meet for dinner that evening at a simpler, more casual place that he would choose.

Sir Gordon sat at his desk in his office waiting for Wallon. Sgt. McDowell had sent reports and photographs on ahead of Owain. Sir Gordon was sitting and studying the photos from the coffins with extreme interest, and also the reports on the murder of Ted Sutter.

"If these are genuine Celtic artifacts, this is an important find. On the private market they could bring large sums of money from collectors. Have the objects removed to an archeology department of a university. The same thing should be done with the old bones. It doesn't appear the bones would be involved in solving a murder in this age. As for the rocks, what do you make of them?" asked Sir William.

"I believe Dr. Glyn Anderson can help us with them, sir," said Owain.

"Let the scientific trade journals pick up the story in one of their articles, and if the news media notices the article and investigates, that is fine," suggested Sir William.

"What concerns me more than anything else," Owain said, "is this gold investment opportunity that Dirk Otis Shedweld is promoting. We can find no information about where he claims to be mining this gold. He uses vague terms; he has blocked our attempt to penetrate his business organization. I have Sergeant McDowell investigating, but he has come up with very few details. I was hoping while here I could pursue Shedweld's interests in London. Superintendent Cadwell strongly recommended caution. He emphasized that Mr. Shedweld has important friends and contacts. Have you heard of this gentleman, sir?"

"Yes, I have, and so have other investors. Shedweld concerns me as well, especially since you have discovered his apparent connection to this case. Duvrey's involvement also bothers me. Presently, he is in Australia. However, I am told he has been seen in the company of this man Shedweld. Several times Duvrey arranged dinner parties, and Shedweld was at them," Sir Gordon said.

Owain said: "What's more, sir, I attended a dinner party at the Ormes Victoria Hotel as the guest of Lord Peter Whitecoft and Sir

Harold Montgomery. After dinner, Tom's wife Gwyneth requested that I escort the ladies from the private dining room to their cottage behind the hotel. It was at that time that Tom observed Shedweld entering the lobby; he pointed him out to me as I left with the ladies. I watched Shedweld enter a private meeting room with Lord Whitecoft and Sir Harold." Owain made note of Sir Gordon's worried reaction to this information.

"I see," Sir Gordon said. "Oh, by the way, my wife and I saw you and Joanna at dinner last night."

"Oh, yes, sir, I expressed to Joanna an interest in asking her out to dinner, she selected the restaurant and made the reservations."

"Well, my boy, I must say you impressed me as a splendid-looking couple. But now back to the case. Your ideas about tracking down Shedweld's company—I approve of this. There are certain people with whom you should talk; and I will give you their names. I am sure I can trust you to be discreet; and my advice is to share and enjoy Joanna's company—but not her confidence. If her father is innocently involved in some sort of illegal business scheme, we must waste no time in bringing this man Shedweld to justice. This financial scheme is taking on a sinister aspect. Good law-abiding people are drawn in, and can lose large amounts of money."

Glyn Anderson's Emotional Breakdown

Owain made reservations for dinner at a casual restaurant he enjoyed when in London. At six o' clock he arrived at Lord Whitecoft's townhouse to pick up Joanna. On their way to the restaurant, Joanna explained that her father had returned that day, and was not happy to find that she had given the servants' time off. He had had to round up his staff and put the house back on his schedule. Owain laughed and encouraged Joanna to relax and enjoy the evening.

"Did you inform him about our plans to go out for dinner tonight? You know fathers can be very strict when it is about their only daughter."

"Yes, I know, but I am over twenty-five, and I can take care of myself. The neighboring servants have already tattled to our servants about last night."

"While you live in your father's house, Joanna, he will be more involved with your life than perhaps you would like." As Owain gently explained.

"Does that mean I should move out, and find my own place? In London that would be expensive, and I am only in London occasionally. I really love to be with my friends in Snowdonia or out at our estate with the horses."

"I can see you enjoy the country life, but for your father's sake, your stirring up the gossiping throngs of London society may upset him."

"You are right," she admitted. "I am too impulsive at times. You see, all I could think about was how you mooned over Francesca that night at the hotel—and she was utterly captivated by you. There I was left out. You didn't notice me, and I was so very much attracted to you. Most of the possible suitors that I have met through family arrangements often turn out to be gay, or have several girlfriends as their trophies. You just swept me away when you spoke with that soft Welsh lilt in your voice, and your elegant intelligent manner. Besides, you do know how handsome you are." Joanna gazed over at him to watch his reaction to her flirtatious but charming frankness.

With a slight blush, Owain responded, "Joanna, I am absolutely captivated by you and my passions are stirred to the point of distraction. You realize that. Expressing my feelings has never been my strong point." He continued: "In fact, for some reason, Francesca and her brother Sir Harold were monopolizing the conversation. When you were sitting at your father's side at dinner that night, I could not help but be aware of you. Francesca is a lovely, fragile young thing; and you are a very stunning young woman. When after dinner Gwyneth entertained us in her cottage sitting room, you were bright, witty, and charming. This case which I am investigating is absorbing almost all my free time." Owain took her hand and pressed her fingers to his lips.

Sitting in a booth, unnoticed by other patrons, Joanna looked at him. After all those ostentatious balls and parties, meeting with all those dull people, she found Owain so special and so appealing. How could she help but fall in love with him? Was she going to be able to convince Owain of that?

Owain looking into Joanna's eyes set his fork down, and took her hand. "Joanna, I found that I have developed very desirous and deep feelings for you. Last night was very special for me. Perhaps next time, we can try and be a little discreet, and not irritate your father by changing the schedules of his household staff."

They exchanged warm romantic looks, and tried to keep their minds on eating. Later, they left the restaurant hand in hand.

While they walked in a nearby park, Owain confessed the reasons to Joanna concerning his reluctance to become involved in a serious relationship. "I have never known a true married parents relationship. My uncle lost his wife shortly after she gave birth to their daughter, Ann. Uncle Hywel had only his sister Catherine to turn to. She saw the need for nurturing the young baby girl, and moved into Gorwyn Hall from her flat at university to take care of the motherless baby. Soon after, my parents were killed in an auto accident. Uncle Hywel and Aunt Catherine were my nearest relatives and brought me to Gorwyn Hall to live with them. I was sent away to school and came back for summers and holidays to Gorwyn Hall. This is the only family that I have known, and I love them very, very much. To consider a marriage has been furthest from my mind at this time.

Joanna listened quietly to Owain. She knew that he was struggling with his feelings; and that he was very serious about their relationship. Owain was not a short fling type of man. This in and of itself drew her even closer to him. Her parents had not had a happy marriage. Theirs had to do with the properness of their stations in their titled social group.

They both decided it would be a good idea to spend the weekend together back in Snowdonia. Owain told her that he had a lot of work to do on the case he was investigating, and he also had an appointment with his neurological surgeon for a checkup tomorrow. Joanna showed immediate concern. She knew about the accident from what Gwyneth had told her. Owain hailed a cab and took Joanna home. He returned to his place—but he missed Joanna the rest of the night.

In the morning, the doctors gave him a thorough going over. They commented about how much more relaxed Owain appeared to be and that he looked a lot healthier. The last time the doctors had seen him, he'd looked very tired. "Whatever it is that you are doing, keep at it," remarked one of his doctors.

After returning to the office, on his desk he found a list of persons that he needs to speak with. Chief Supt. Gordon had made appointments for him with prominent bankers and businessmen. Owain was out all day talking to these prominent individuals about Dirk Otis Shedweld's business connections and finances. The confidential comments that were made about this man concerned his ability to be very cunning, sharp, and "not to be trusted." Owain was alarmed and wondered how Shedweld had been able to entangle Lord Whitecoft and Sir Montgomery in his scheme? Of course, Wallon never mentioned their names while conversing with the contacts that Gordon sent him to meet.

Mulling the information over in his mind, he was bothered that this cunning businessman had gained these men's confidences by promising fat returns to his investors who lent him money to locate lost gold mines. Someone had introduced Whitecoft and Montgomery to Shedweld? There must be a missing link here. Was Duvrey involved? Owain pondered this possibility on his way back to his office. After meeting with Chief Supt. Gordon, he still was not sure who the contact was that Shedweld had used to ensnare Lord Whitecoft and Sir Harold in his deceitful misuse of investments. Owain wanted to follow-up on this investigation. Sir William Gordon advised him to be careful. Both Lord Whitecoft and Harold Hadley are his close friends. He wanted to keep their names confidential.

Upon returning to his place that night he found a message on his answering machine from Joanna saying that she had returned to her girlfriend's flat in Snowdonia. She left the number where she could be reached, and mentioned that upon leaving, her father had come up to her room to say goodbye. He gave her a hug and pulled affectionately on her chin as he said, "Owain is a special young man, and I like him."Owain hit the replay button a couple of times to listen to the message again. Joanna had become a very important part of his life now. He thought of his uncle and aunt. They would be surprised and, he hoped, happy. He packed his clothes for the weekend and probably longer. The case in Snowdonia was going to take a lot of his time. Little did he realize this case was about to take a serious turn that would affect both Joanna and his future?

McDowell contacted him that night about the surveillance of Shedweld's cottage. Evidently, the police officer who had been in the cave when Older and Denton were carrying boxes of objects and bones out to their vehicles had recognized seeing the two men again at the cottage as they came and went during the night. McDowell had shot pictures with his infra-red camera of cars and of the men, including John Older and Bill Denton. They followed the two men down to the harbor, where they took a high speed launch out to a large freighter, and stayed the night. That explained why the people in the town did not see them during the day. Later, McDowell said that he watched divers go out on a launch to search for the coffins. After discovering that the coffins were not there any longer, the divers hastily returned to their launch and took off.

Back at the cave, Anderson's team conducting the archeology dig was continuing their operation, according to McDowell. They returned one morning to find that a hole had been dug at one side of the cave away from the dig. It was quite deep and piles of dirt were scattered everywhere onto the dig sight. What had been in the new hole, no one knew. Most likely, more Celtic relics were taken. Again the cave had been vandalized. McDowell noticed that a ladder had been used to climb up to the opening that led out to the ledge where Anderson had gone to bring back the police during the time when they were all locked in the cave. Going around to the ledge again, Glyn Anderson and McDowell climbed up to the place where Tom Lewis had located the bodies in the cave.

Glyn cried, *"Oh no, the gold has been torn from her. Mother Earth, I shall avenge this damage to you!"* McDowell didn't know what to make of Glyn's sudden emotional outburst. He had never been up to the ledge before.

McDowell explained to Owain, "Anderson continued to be very upset and ranted and raved around the spot where he had found the small vein of gold. Anderson had spotted the vein, he told me on the surface of the rock ledge when he was with you that first day." McDowell continued: "I took pictures of the side of the cliff and ledge. He crawled back into the cave from the ledge opening and climbed down to leave the others watching him in amazement. His associates, Brian Holmes and Edward Grant, told me that they had never seen Glyn so upset. He left displaying an emotional rage. They explained that Anderson was generally a quiet person." McDowell finished by saying, "I will have the pictures for you to study when you return to Snowdonia, sir."

Owain boarded the first train to Wales the next morning. McDowell met him at the station. They returned to the hotel near police headquarters. District Superintendent Cadwell was waiting to meet them along with Detective Jones, who had information he had gathered on the ship anchored out a ways from shore. It was a freighter, about to leave on a long trip to several ports, one of which was located on the east coast of the United States. Lorries had been spotted the day before parked at the cottage at Shedweld's, loading boxes from the cottage's interior. Owain was afraid that this meant they were about to make a run for it. He told McDowell to check out Shedweld's salvage-yard business, and also his other offices in Liverpool, to see if the same activities were occurring in these places. They must be attempting to escape the country in the freighter.

Owain was convinced that they must file for a warrant to bring John Older and Bill Denton in for questioning concerning the death of Ted Sutter. These two must not have a chance to escape on the freighter. The contractor, Sam Conrad, had returned. The police wanted answers to their questions concerning his involvement with Shedweld's business dealings. It was Conrad's employee who had been strangled down by the wharf. A warrant for the search of the cottage must be obtained. Time was running out. Dirk Otis Shedweld may have already set in motion his arrangements to disappear. Owain could see that Superintendent Cadwell was ill at ease and nervous, but agreed that this action was needed.

Right after noon while they were at Cadwell's office an emergency call came in to Police headquarters. It was reported that Glyn Anderson had been found shot to death in his flat. A young woman was being held by the local constable for possibly being responsible for shooting him. Wallon, McDowell, Jones, and Cadwell rushed out to their police cars and made their way to the scene. Forensics was also notified, as was pathology.

Upon arriving on the scene, they found two police cars already there; and already, a small crowd had gathered. Owain jumped out of his car and ran up the stairs to Glyn's flat. Crumpled on the floor was the body; a bullet had penetrated the side of his head. Sitting on a chair with the constable nearby was Joanna Whitecoft. Her shirt and slacks were covered with blood. She looked up and ran over to Owain.

"Glyn wanted to shoot himself! I tried to stop him. We struggled with his gun; and it went off towards his head. He fell to the floor. I tried to stop the bleeding from his head wound. *I couldn't stop the bleeding, I couldn't stop the bleeding! Oh! Owain, he didn't want to live,"* cried Joanna. "He kept saying, "Now, I can be with Mother Earth forever." Joanna started trembling; Owain could see she was going into shock.

"Call an ambulance. Bring over the doctor; she is in shock, and needs care immediately," he ordered. Then, Owain put her head down gently and lifted her feet up on to his rolled-up jacket.

The constable came over to Superintendent Cadwell and explained. "We found her on the floor with the victim, holding his head in her lap. The gun was in her other hand. We searched for a suicide note and couldn't find one."

Ambulance attendants entered the room, lifted Joanna on to a stretcher, and left for hospital. Owain talked with McDowell. Superintendent Cadwell was giving orders to his forensic team. Everyone put on latex gloves to investigate the crime scene. The pathologist was bent over the body of Glyn Anderson. The pistol was secured in a sealed evident bag. The fingerprint experts had arrived. Blood samples were being taken, and the investigation of the crime scene was well underway. The crowd of people and reporters that had gathered watched as Joanna was lifted into the ambulance. The Anderson's body would be removed to the morgue later.

"Sir," said McDowell to Owain, "Maybe it would be best to go over to the hospital." Owain's face showed great concern. Owain realized that Joanna was in serious trouble unless they could confirm Anderson's suicide.

Cadwell came over to Owain. He said in an official tone of voice, "She spoke to you before she passed out. What did she say?"

"Joanna Whitecoft told me that she tried to prevent Glyn Anderson from killing himself, and in the struggle the gun went off. I will be making a formal written report of her exact words and give you a copy." Owain responded in the same official tone of voice.

"The local constable who was the first on the scene reported to me that she was mumbling something about suicide, the same thing she said to you just now. Will you be contacting Lord Peter Whitecoft concerning his daughter's being a suspect in this murder investigation?"

A tensed expression appeared on Owain's grey face. McDowell looked down at his boss's clenched, white-knuckled fist, and realized his chief inspector was about to take a swing at Cadwell. At this time, it was a suicide or accident case. Cadwell was jumping to conclusions.

In a calm voice, McDowell thoughtfully suggested that it would be perhaps best for Chief Inspector Wallon to go back to the police station to make his phone calls. He probably would want to apprise Chief Superintendent Gordon about what had happened. Owain's clenched fist relaxed. He turned to McDowell with a grim look, and said. "You are right Clyde I should contact Sir Gordon immediately, thanks for the suggestion." They both left the crime scene.

Before reporting to headquarters, however, Owain and McDowell went to the hospital where Joanna Whitecoft had been taken. She was found to be in a state of shock and the doctor had administered a sedative, which would keep her under until morning. At that time the doctors thought she would be ready to answer questions. A police guard was stationed outside her room to keep reporters away. Acting upon Owain's urgent call, Lord Peter had sent word that he would be there as soon as possible.

Wallon walked into district police headquarters with Sgt. McDowell. They found the place deserted except for the desk sergeant. Again, the question was raised in both their minds as to why Superintendent Cadwell was leaving the station without his attendance. He should have returned to take care of headquarters business. Most of the staff at the station was out on the murder investigation. Others were involved in the everyday business outside of headquarters. Suddenly, the desk phone rang, and the sergeant answered. A second murder had taken place. Constable Morgan at the village of Dewi Sant, where Shedweld's cottage was located was calling Cadwell for an investigation team. The sergeant's voice could be heard speaking with constable. Then, the sergeant turned towards Wallon and McDowell and in an excited voice announced that Mr. Dirk Otis Shedweld had been found shot in his driveway. The desk sergeant was concerned as to who could respond. This year staff at district headquarters had been severely cut back for lack of funds from the government. There was no one of detective status available to send over to this new crime scene.

"Sergeant, we will respond," stated chief inspector Wallon.

Wallon and McDowell took off for Shedweld's cottage immediately. The neighboring village constable met them at the driveway, and showed them up to the crime scene, then returned to his post to keep everyone away. McDowell took one look at the corpse, and from what he observed Shedweld had been shot as he entered his car. There were no footprints in the gravel next to the car. However, there were tire tracks where a car had turned around and went back down the driveway.

Wallon questioned the villagers waiting at the bottom of the driveway about a car that they might have seen earlier. Did they see a person leaving the cottage in a hurry? One of the villagers told them that he had seen a car drive in and heard what he thought was a car back firing. He ran up the driveway and saw someone in workman's clothes jump into a Land Rover. The vehicle almost hit him as it drove down the road. He could not give a better description than that.

"Do you know what time it was when you saw the Land Rover?" asked Wallon.

"No, but early, during the morning, I'm not exactly sure of the time."

"Give your name to the constable and we will talk with you later," said Wallon.

There was no gun found in the area. The location was taped off by Constable Morton and a constable from a neighboring village.

Owain's cell phone rang as he and McDowell were searching for more evidence. Chief Supt. William Gordon was calling. Owain was told that Lord Whitecoft was at the hospital, and his private lawyer was with him. Lord Whitecoft wanted to speak with Owain as soon as possible. Owain told Sir Gordon to take Lord Whitecoft over to The Ormes Victoria Hotel. The newspaper press was already like mad dogs, roaming the scene at the hospital. The police and the doctors could protect Joanna, and he would see Lord Whitecoft at the hotel. Sir Gordon agreed, and said that they would be there. Owain then called Tom and explained what had happened and asked him to find private rooms for Gordon, Whitecoft, and the lawyer. Owain left McDowell with the constables. He gave him instructions to keep the crime scene at the cottage secure as he drove off to the hotel.

Was It Suicide or Murder

Leaving McDowell at Shedweld's cottage, Owain drove in the Scotland Yard's Land Rover at breakneck speed over to the hotel to meet with Sir Gordon and Lord Whitecoft. Tom was outside when Owain drove up. As Owain jumped out of the Land Rover, he tossed the car keys to Tom.

"My luggage is in the back, Tom. Have the others arrived?"

"Yes, Owain, they are upstairs in the hotel suite. Fortunately it was free. Do you want to go straight up? I can have your luggage put in the cottage with me if you like."

"Yes, Yes, Tom, please do. I'm going on up. Watch for the newspaper press, they may be on their way. Try to ward them off."

"How is Joanna?" Tom asked.

"She has been given a strong sedative which should last until morning. Cadwell, the bastard, assumes that it is a murder case and not a suicide. Why? I don't know. The constable, who was first on the scene, heard Joanna explain that Glyn was attempting to shoot himself in the head in an attempt . She grabbed for the pistol in Glyn's hand, and it went off. She told me the same thing. The police have not found a note to verify it was a suicide. Tell me, where is the motive for murder? Why would Joanna kill him?"

"Do you think that they have enough evidence to hold her on suspicion, or just to detain her for questioning?" Tom asked.

Owain shook his head. "I don't know."

Then he blurted out the next terrible news. "Shedweld has been shot in his driveway as he was trying to get away. When the local constable called in the crime, the district police headquarters was so short handed they had no one to send out to Shedweld's murder scene. McDowell is out there now at the crime scene with only a couple of local constables to assist in the investigation. How can the district station be so shorthanded? Why was Cadwell not at his own police station? I have to go upstairs to meet with Sir Gordon."

Owain left Tom and made for the elevator. He got off at the top floor. Sir Gordon was standing in the doorway to the suite. Lord Peter Whitecoft was sitting on the divan inside, and his lawyer was at the desk, on the phone. Lord Peter's face was strained as he looked up and smiled at Owain when he entered.

"Brief us on what you know, Owain," spoke Sir Gordon in a serious voice.

Owain walked quickly into the parlor as he struggled to gain control over himself. Lord Peter introduced his lawyer, Malcolm Townsend. They sat around the table in the parlor and listened as Owain went over the details of the last six hours, starting with Sgt. McDowell's meeting him at the train station that morning. McDowell reported on the information he had gathered the day before from the surveillance of Shedweld's cottage, also about meeting up with Glyn at the cave, where Anderson suddenly became enraged by the excavation of the gold ore from the hill side.

Today, before Cadwell could request a warrant for the search of Shedweld's cottage and other places, the phone call came in to Cadwell's office from the constable in Bangor. Evidently someone on the street heard a gunshot coming from the flat above. The constable went up to investigate. Upon opening the door, he found Glyn lying dead on the floor. Then, Owain went on to explain what had happened when he, Cadwell, and McDowell arrived at the flat. Joanna had been found by the constable at the scene of Glyn's death when he arrived. Supt. Cadwell inferred that he was not convinced that Glyn had committed suicide and that Joanna had shot him. Owain shook his head in disbelief with emotion showing in his voice. We returned to the district station. Upon arriving at the district police station, the sergeant on duty was on the phone receiving an emergence call from Constable Morton of Dewi Sant village where Shedweld's cottage was located. Shedweld was dead. His body was found by the side of his car in the driveway. The entire detective staff from Cadwell's police station was still collecting evidence at Glyn Anderson's flat. He and McDowell drove out to the Dewi Sant crime sight. After doing preliminary investigations of this new crime scene, Owain told them he left for his meeting here at The Ormes Victoria hotel.

Sir Gordon complimented Owain on his quick and responsible action but recommended that he return to the new crime scene. "Go over to Dewi Sant village and take charge. I know that it should be Superintendent Cadwell's district. Call this Superintendent Cadwell. Tell him that you should be conducting the initial investigation with his team at the Shedweld's cottage. I know that it is his jurisdiction. They must lock down the new murder site at the village. Lord Peter and Malcolm Townsend plan to stay the night with her. I am going to stay here, and I'll contact the port authority to hold the freighter for a customs search. I will need several government department authorities to stop the freighter from leaving these waters. If your suspicion is correct, they have people with stolen valuables on board; and we need to hold them accountable for removing these items from England."

Owain went down to Tom's cottage and changed his clothes. He explained to Tom about the plans for the night. Tom was shaken by the news concerning Joanna's collapse and the suspicion that she may have murdered Glyn. He wanted to give his support to his friend; the seriousness of the various crimes that had taken place during such a short time period was very troubling to Tom. As Owain drove off again, Tom looked anxiously after him. His friend was pushed to the limit; and Tom did not know how he could help him. He was no longer an inspector with Scotland Yard. Gwyneth was in America with Francesca and James Montgomery. They were not planning on returning for another week or so. Should he call her in America to tell her what had happened to Joanna? Tom thought it would be better to wait. Right now he was most concerned about Owain and the nasty blow to the head that he had suffered when his car rolled over the side of the road. Who were those guys who had been dynamiting the hillside? Were they connected to this case?

Owain called detective inspector Jones from his cell phone in his car phone.

"I have been trying to reach Cadwell. Is he there with you?" Owain asked urgently.

"No, he left some time ago," responded detective inspector Jones.

"I left a message on his cell phone about the murder at Dewi Sant. Did he get my message?" Owain asked Jones with mounting frustration in his voice. . . . *"The murder at Shedweld's cottage?*

"No, not that I have heard," responded Jones surprised. "What is this all about?"

Owain quickly explained to Jones what had happened to Shedweld, and that he was on his way to the village of Dewi Sant now.

"Are there members of the forensic team at the Anderson crime scene? Send them out to Shedweld's cottage. You must locate Cadwell immediately, Jones," demanded Owain. "The crime scene has only two constables and my sergeant to do the investigation. Send your team or replacements from another police headquarters." Owain was impatient.

"I am leaving for our district headquarters right now; and I will have the team who is still here leave for Dewi Sant. They are mostly finished, and the body of Glyn Anderson has been taken to the morgue. I will see the evidence put on a van, and taken back to headquarters. As soon as I reach Superintendent Cadwell, I will call you." Jones signed off hurriedly, leaving Owain wondering to himself about this sign of mismanagement at Cadwell's police station.

When Owain reached Dewi Sant, most of the townspeople were gathered in front of the driveway that led up to Shedweld's cottage. A constable was holding back the onlookers as Wallon drove up.

"They are up at the cottage, sir," The constable said.

"I will leave my car here constable and walk the rest of the way. Here are the keys if you have to move my car."

As Owain walked up the driveway, his cell phone was ringing. A very worried Detective Inspector Jones was calling him.

"We can't locate Superintendent Cadwell. He doesn't answer his cell phone. The remaining constable at headquarters doesn't know where he is. I called his home, and there is no answer. I am leaving now to go to his home and will find out why no one is answering the telephone. Call you back soon." Jones tells Owain.

Suspicion was growing in Owain's mind. Cadwell had always been reluctant about talking to or asking questions of Shedweld. For what reason would he avoid returning my call unless something had happened to him? If there had been a car accident, the police station would have been notified. Where is Cadwell?

Owain was met by Sergeant McDowell at the front door of the cottage. The constable was out guarding the body, and McDowell had gone inside to look around to see if there was anyone else in the house. McDowell was brought up to date on Sir Gordon's orders. Owain told McDowell that no one knew what had happened to Cadwell.

Owain's cell phone rang again. A very disturbed Detective Inspector Jones was on the line.

"Chief Inspector Wallon, we entered Superintendent Cadwell's home. His wife was not there, but she had left her husband a note saying that she was leaving him for good. We found Cadwell drunk and passed out at the kitchen table with the note in his hand. I am heading back to headquarters, but first I must round up everyone with experience who can help at the scene. We will head up to Dewi Sant right away." Jones signed off.

Ten minutes later, Owain's cell phone rang again. It was Jones on the line. "Sorry to report Wallon, the security closet at headquarters has been broken into. All the treasure items in the boxes have been removed. Only the boxes containing the stones are left. The constable who was on duty told us that he knows of no one going down there. The forensic team discovered the break-in when they returned with the evidence from Anderson's flat. What do you want me to do?" A stunned Jones asked Owain. The only key to the security room was supposed to be in Cadwell procession.

"Immediately, lock up all the evidence from the Anderson crime scene in another security room. Put a guard at the door. The security room which had been broken into is now a crime scene," stated Owain. "We must conduct a search for evidence concerning who was responsible for stealing the valuable items."

"The team and I will leave headquarters as soon as we have secured the area," said Jones in a strained voice. The reputation of his headquarters was damaged. His respect for Cadwell his boss was shaken. The police officers were a close-knit team and this brought their senior officer's responsibility into question.

Owain told McDowell what had happened. McDowell shrugged and asked for orders—it was going to be a long night.

By daybreak the combined teams of Jones and another district's forensic team finished their investigation of the Shedweld crime scene. Shedweld's body was removed to the morgue. The scene was properly taped off. The reporters were given a statement by Chief Inspector Owain Wallon with Detective Inspector Jones at his side. Nothing more could be done on this site. Reports would be written and logged in later. The very tired and worn out police teams headed home.

"Where do we go from here, sir?" asked McDowell.

"Well, McDowell, you look like you could use some rest. Are you still registered at the hotel near headquarters? If you are, I suggest you go and grab some sleep. Inspector Jones looks like he is going to do the same thing. As far as Cadwell is concerned, it is out of our hands. The official police authorities in Wales have been notified and will investigate the superintendent's drunkenness on duty case from here. I am heading back to Tom's cottage next and then probably over to the hospital. Can I give you a lift?"

"No, sir, Detective Inspector Jones will do that, "responded McDowell.

After he returned to The Ormes Victoria Hotel, Owain talked with Tom over an early breakfast and coffee. It had been a grueling twenty-four hours. Sir George was up in the hotel's suite. Owain left a message for him about the investigation's progress. He of course also reported that Cadwell had been out of touch and was found drunk in his kitchen; and his wife had left him. The security closet had been broken into at the police station and the valuables taken. Tom advised Owain to grab a nap before heading out again.

A couple of hours later, a call came in for Owain to join Sir Gordon upstairs in Lord Peter's suite. Dressing quickly, Owain made his way over to the hotel and up to the top floor. When he arrived, he found Malcolm Townshend and Sir Gordon talking in the parlor of the suite. Lord Peter was sleeping. They had brought

Joanna back with them. Townsend had convinced the authorities that they could not hold Joanna without more evidence at this time. A thorough search should be made for a suicide note, or a motive for Glyn's murder established before they could consider an arrest warrant for Joanna. Owain was visibly relieved. Joanna, who looked stressed and worn out, was standing at the bedroom doorway. She made her way over to Owain and grabbed him. The other two men quietly left the room.

"You are my brave knight. Thank goodness you were there. I have brought back your jacket. I am sorry; it is stained. We are returning to father's estate soon. I think that I can rest there. Please come see me. I think that I am in love with you. Maybe you are in love with me?" She raised her face with its dark-circled eyes and looked up at Owain.

"Oh, Joanna, of course I am. I will come to see you, hopefully soon. I'm afraid this case is going to take even more of my time than before. We must prove that you had nothing to do with Glyn's death. I am not sure that they will allow me to continue to officially work on this case. However, I will not stop until we have some answers and clear your name."

Standing out of earshot, Malcolm Townsend, indicating Owain, asked if that was the man who had been at the restaurant in London with Joanne. Sir Gordon nodded yes.

"He is a policeman," remarked Townsend.

"So am I, Malcolm," said Sir Gordon curtly.

Townsend realized his mistake, and they turned to approach the couple. Sir Gordon apologized to Joanna, "I'm afraid that Owain and I have very important business to discuss. I know that your father plans to leave shortly."

Sir Gordon and Owain went into another room to talk. Sir Gordon told him, "The freighter slipped out to sea before we could stop her. The first port of entry was Le Havre on the French coast, and the police authority there will conduct a search that you can attend. You would have to leave for France immediately. Sergeant McDowell and Inspector Landers from our branch will continue the investigation here. As for Superintendent Cadwell, it was believed that he also had been an investor in Shedweld's illegal financial scheme. This will probably cost him his position at police headquarters. It has been suggested that Detective Jones will be promoted to replace Cadwell as superintendent.

"When you reach the port in France you must contact Police Inspector Jean Fussard. You can present your papers to him. I have been told that more of the treasure was stolen from the Wales district headquarters. Take with you all the photographs and reports that you need. The British council at Le Havre will be there to meet you. Hopefully it will not take long. Do you have any questions?"

"No, sir."

"Then, good luck," said Superintendent Sir Gordon.

Owain returned to the hotel near district headquarters. Sgt. McDowell had just arrived in Owain's room. Owain told McDowell that Gordon was putting Inspector Landers on the case and that he would be arriving soon; he also told him of his assignment to Le Havre. They hoped to make a thorough search of the ship for stolen items with a warrant for John Olden and Bill Denton. The two men were to be held at London headquarters.

"I'm not sure what my responsibilities will be concerning the investigation into the death of Glyn Anderson and Dirk Otis Shedweld after I have returned from France. I plan to be kept up to date on the findings until I am told otherwise. You know how to reach me in France; and I would like to hear from you daily. Keep an eye on those security rooms and the evidence inside them. Inspector Landers is a good man; he won't make the mistakes that Duvrey did."

Sgt. McDowell said that he would keep Owain informed of developments. They had enjoyed working together. McDowell would miss his chief inspector, whom he considered to be the very best that the special branch of Scotland Yard had. McDowell vowed that he and Landers would get to the bottom of all this. The discharged superintendent Cadwell must have more to do with this case; and he intended to find out what the connection was between Shedweld and Cadwell because he was sure that there was one.

Chief Inspector Wallon Leaves for France

The following morning, after chief Inspector Wallon had left for France, Sgt. McDowell, with Inspector Landers, who had arrived the previous night, headed over to district headquarters for their first meeting with acting replacement for Superintendent Cadwell. Floyd Jones was taking over the duties of investigating the case. The discharged Superintendent Cadwell was under house arrest for drunkenness while on duty. McDowell and Tom Landers entered the briefing room and were greeted by the new Supt. Jones with a broad smile. The others watched them take a seat up front.

McDowell studied the briefing charts. On the left-hand chart, the names of the present suspects were to be listed. McDowell, with a growing feeling of apprehension, noticed that the only name yet listed was *Lady Joanna Whitecoft as a suspect in the two murder cases*: Shedweld and Anderson. The other names were John Older and Bill Denton, with warrants listed next to their names as suspects for the other two murder cases: Ted Sutter and the strangled workman. In parentheses was listed Prof. Glyn Anderson as a possible suicide. Below each name, space was left for information such as alibis in each case for the named suspects. Three more charts were in a row with the name of the victim at the top. A separate chart was assigned for each victim and much of the details of the individual crimes were on each chart.

After everyone had taken their seats, Jones spoke to the officers. "I welcome the assistance of the neighboring police stations in releasing four more officers to work on the investigation of these crimes. I especially welcome the assistance of the special branch of Scotland Yard, who are involved in the investigation of these cases." There was a slight shuffling of the policemen's feet.

Jones continued, "As you can see by the charts, and the reports that you received when you entered this room, we have a formidable investigation here. My plan is to have four teams made up of one officer from our district and one from the surrounding districts, to investigate each of the murder cases. The inspector and the sergeant from Scotland Yard will be with me investigating all the cases. If there are no questions, I would advise you to take the time this morning to go over all the reports on these cases, not just the one that you are assigned to." It was now obvious that newly promoted to acting Superintendent Floyd Jones was in full charge of the cases.

Jones asked Landers and McDowell to join him in his new office. As they entered, McDowell realized that everything connected to the former Superintendent Cadwell had been removed. He remembered seeing quite a few awards on the walls before; these were now gone.

"Just now, I have been notified that Chief Inspector Wallon has been successful in arresting John Older and Bill Denton in France. They are on the way to Scotland Yard. Also being returned are the packing cases with the special Celtic pieces and gold coins that were stolen from our secured closet, along with many other pieces as well as quantities of pure gold ore. It is my understanding that Older and Denton will be questioned at Scotland Yard headquarters and then brought over to us." McDowell and Landers were pleased.

The three of them spent the rest of the morning reviewing all the evidence collected from the four murder cases: the strangled workman, Ted Sutter, Glyn Anderson, and Shedweld. New pieces of evidence that had been collected within the last twenty-four hours were discussed. In the afternoon, McDowell would be taking Landers to the main murder sites, and to the cave. They grabbed something to eat and took off.

Before leaving, McDowell and Landers wanted to review the charges against Lady Joanna Whitecoft. What was the evidence against her in the cases of Anderson and Shedweld? Supt. Jones told them that this suspect has no verifiable alibi for the times of the murders.

"Questioned witnesses have told us that she does have experience with the use of guns. Her friends who she stays with went out early and did not see her all day. Neighbors outside of Anderson's flat saw her enter, and then heard a shot. Another witness claims that they saw someone driving Anderson's car as it left from behind his flat early in the morning. When asked if they could describe the driver, they weren't sure who it was. Anderson's car was later found parked behind his flat. The suspect's prints were found in the car on the driver's side. The last time that Joanna can be positively identified was the night before at a meeting of the environmentalists club.

Two shots had been fired from the gun that was taken from the crime scene at Anderson's flat. The gun that killed Shedweld was the same caliber as the one that killed Anderson according to the crime labs examination report." The forensic staffed reported that two bullets had been secured as evidence after being extracted from the bodies of Anderson and Shedweld. The bullets match the caliber of the gun which had been fired twice found at the Anderson crime scene. No gun was found at the Shedweld crime scene. Nothing more was said about the evidence.

McDowell sat listening to Jones, and reflected upon the evidence presented against Lady Joanna Whitecoft. The one thing that stood out in his mind was that there was not a clear-cut motive. Jones proposed his explanation as to how Joanna could have had time to go out in the morning to kill Shedweld. She would have returned to confront Glyn Anderson with what she had done. But this did not seem reasonable to McDowell and Landers. Cadwell had been the first officer to suggest that Joanna had killed Anderson. Now, here was Jones taking up Cadwell's accusation, and adding Shedweld's murder to the case that he was building against Joanna to Landers or McDowell. Why was Jones insisting on putting Lady Joanna's name forward as the suspect? Why center the investigation on her alone? After all, the contractor, Sam Conrad, could have been involved. McDowell asked Jones if they had interviewed Conrad and was told, "Not yet."

Back in London, two officers were assigned to take Older and Denton to North Wales the following morning. Owain knew that Older and Denton were the two closest links that they had to Shedweld's illegal activities. Sir Gordon wanted to have an opportunity to question them first, and Chief Inspector Wallon was included in the examination of Older and Denton. They resisted interrogation and demanded legal representation.

Chief Inspector Wallon had requested to be allowed to return to Wales and the investigation there. Sir Gordon explained that he wanted Owain to take some time off. This would be a temporary removal of Owain from active participation in this case for personal reasons only. Sir William suggested that Owain could return to Gorwyn Hall for the weekend. Owain understood and accepted his advice. This would not preclude him from staying in touch with McDowell. Sir Willliam told him. After Wallon had left Gordon's office, his staff man, Stuart, entered and asked if it was wise to let Owain travel to Wales where he would be so close to Joanna Whitecoft. Sir Gordon gazed towards Stuart and said he appreciated Stuart's question, then advised him to let well enough alone.

At Gorwyn Hall, a Land Rover pulled up and stopped at the front entrance. Two women got out. Gwyneth was back in Wales from her trip to America. She had left Francesca with Gwyneth's parents in the United States. Evidently her brother Guy and Francesca were dating. James had returned to his brother's place in England.

Once inside, Gwyneth introduced Joanna Whitecoft to Uncle Hywel.

"Come in, ladies. We have tea and biscuits waiting. Aunt Catherine has left for the train station to meet Owain and should be back in a while." said Hywel.

Gwyneth enjoyed her tea, but said she must soon go to the hotel, where Tom was busy with a full roster of hotel guests. Hywel encouraged her not to leave too soon. As he explained to her, "No one must think that you are here only to bring a lady with you. Our neighbors can be nosy sometimes."

Gwyneth called Tom goes to the telephone to explain to Tom-to tell him that she would not be back until late. Tom agreed that she should stay there for a while.

Soon they heard Catherine's Bentley coming up the driveway and continue on around to the garage in the back. Elena and her daughter Agnes were staying in the village with friends. Before she left, Elena had prepared lamb stew, her specialty. It was ready to serve, plus other quick and easy meals.

Owain and his aunt entered by the back door. Hywel greeted Owain, who looked around for Elena and Agnes because he could smell the aroma of Elena's famous lamb stew.

"Where are Elena and Agnes?" he asked his aunt.

"They are in town with friends."

Uncle Hywel encouraged Owain to go on into the drawing room and said they would follow. Becoming suspicious about what was going on, Owain walked into the drawing room—and straight into Joanna's arms. Gwyneth quietly left for the kitchen. After a few minutes, Aunt Catherine could wait no longer and headed for the drawing room to meet Joanna Whitecoft, the young lady she had been hearing so much about.

Owain introduced his aunt. "I would like you to meet my aunt Catherine, and I guess you have already been introduced to my uncle Hywel."

"It is such a pleasure to meet you, Joanna, after all that Gwyneth has told us about you."

"Oh! Aunt Catherine, it is wonderful to meet you, and thank you for having me here under these circumstances."

"Not at all, we are delighted to have you here," said Hywel with a broad smile on his face. "I have brought up some very nice wine from our cellar. Shall we have a toast?"

Hywel had the glasses on the table and was already pouring the wine when Owain, blushing a little, said, "Let's not rush things, Uncle, please."

"I mean a toast to our good fortune to have the chance to see you here again, Owain. My my, what else did you think I meant?" Everyone laughed and joked about how Owain was being kidded by his uncle.

After dinner, Gwyneth went out to her car and drove back to Tom and their cottage at the hotel. Tom was waiting for her, ready to hear all about the big surprise.

Hywel and Catherine made their own excuses and went off to their rooms. Owain poured two snifters of brandy and joined Joanna on the couch.

"Please, Joanna, I must speak with you, and it cannot be in my official capacity, because I may be called in to work on the murder cases again. But as a man who truly loves you, I want to remove this false criminal accusation from your life. I must ask you to help me. What we discuss cannot be put forwarded to this case from me. I must find another intermediary. I don't want to be called to the witness stand. There are ways that I can help you. First, Glyn was a fine person who must have gone crazy. If he meant to commit suicide, from what I know about suicides, the party wants to leave a message behind. Could you have come in before he had a chance to write a suicide note? Maybe Glyn realized that you were going to try to stop him and just went through with his plan to shoot himself, and did not have time for the note? If this is the case, then we must find some other evidence where he talked about his feelings for ending his life."

Joanna sat very quietly next to him on the sofa when a thought occurred to her. "Yes, there might be something that we could find. Have they searched his locker and desk at the lab? He kept a journal about his work, but also, I believe he wrote down other personal thoughts. As you know, I was very fond of Glyn. He had such a wonderful, kind nature. He deeply believed in this beautiful earth of ours that he referred to as "Mother Earth." Every time he would hear about mines or deforestation, Glyn would become upset, and refer to the act as killing Mother Earth. I know he didn't believe in God because we talked about it. He worshipped Mother Earth and her beauty. I guess you can say he was obsessed with his beliefs. He prayed to her and worshiped her. He never would even cut a flower—that was desecration. Maybe he went crazy when he saw what Ted Sutter had done in the cave. . . . I don't know. He used to talk about Shedweld and his mining plans. This was very disturbing, he would say."

Owain listened intently. He remembered something Glyn had said about Mother Earth.

"Do you know anything about his owning a pistol? Usually people with beliefs like his would not own any type of gun."

"He did refer to a pistol once, when he said that he abhorred physical violence and that he was afraid that to save Mother Earth, he would have to stop the desecrators with a deadly weapon. But I never thought he meant it, until I saw him in his room with the pistol. He was pointing it at his own head, and saying, 'Now I must come to you, Mother Earth. I have killed the others who were harming you. I am not strong enough to continue killing.'" said Joanna about what Glyn had confided to her.

"Others?" Owain asked. "What do you think he meant by 'others'?"

"I'm not sure," said Joanna.

"His locker at the lab must be searched. Hopefully, you are right, and there is enough information there for the court to remove the murder charge and consider suicide," said Owain. "How much has your father told you about his investments with Shedweld?"

"Not very much—he knew how I felt about mining."

"Do you have any idea who approached your father about talking to Shedweld?"

"Of course I do. It was that high-society adulteress, Lady Duvrey, she was his on-again, off-again mistress." Joanna said this with a cynical tone in her voice.

"Now, why would Lord Peter have an affair with that old lady?"

"Oh! Owain, you don't understand do you? When she was younger, she was very strikingly attractive. Then as she aged, so did her lovers. They grew old together, and she knew how to make the most of her aging charm. Older men like my father want to be charmed in the ways that they have been accustomed to through the years. They don't want a young, voluptuous woman who probably makes jokes to her friends about her elderly suitors behind their backs. They want the comfortable, charming one to whom they have become accustomed. She had many, many suitors and they all knew about each other and just passed it off at the club as the way things are," explained Joanna.

"My mother was the daughter of a duke, and died some time ago. She produced two sons, then I came along. Having more children was not what she wanted, so if her husband went around with lovers, that was all . That would be alright by her. As long as he was discreet and no serious gossip started. Many children were born to dukes outside their marriages. That is why Louis Duvrey was taken care of. For instance, Henry VIII had an illegitimate son who lived and later received a title as earl of Richmond. However, he could not inherit the throne."

"By the way," Joanna looked over at Owain. "I know why people seem to recognize you. There is a portrait in a certain portrait gallery located on the country estate of a famous duke. You are very fortunate to have his features. He was brilliant and highly regarded for his bravery in World War II."

"Please, let's stop fantasizing about who I resemble, and return to talking about Glyn, and how to change the charge of murder to death by suicide," Owain said impatiently.

"How can I be charged with murder? I had no reason to kill Glyn; he was like a brother to me."

"Unfortunately, there is another reason. You could have been protecting your father from Shedweld and killed him also. Glyn found out, and you had to kill him."

"What? That is crazy."

"Where were you when Shedweld was killed? Have you been asked for an alibi for that time?"

"Why, yes, the authorities are checking into that now."

"Shedweld was shot earlier in the day, before you found Glyn about to commit suicide. The claim is that the bullets came from the same pistol—the one found in your hand when the constable entered Glyn's flat. People saw you arrive at Glyn's place, but they did not see Glyn leave earlier, and said that he had apparently been there all day. Shedweld's murderer apparently drove Glyn's car and used his pistol. No one can identify the person driving Glyn's car. However, they found your prints in Glyn's car."

"I have driven Glyn's car in the past; so my prints would be there."

"Your prints were not found on Shedweld's, car and neither were Glyn's. Obviously, the killer never touched Shedweld's car but shot him outside, near the car. What did you tell the police about your movements during the early part of the day?"

"That is the problem. I really didn't see any people that day. I slept late at my girlfriend's flat. She had gone out hiking with friends. I made breakfast, and then started to work on the latest minutes of our environmental group's meeting from the night before. Glyn's flat is just down the road. I walked over to ask him if he wanted to go hiking." said Joanna.

"Did you receive any cell phone calls or wave to anyone on the street? Did you stop to get something to eat?"

"No, I thought maybe Glyn and I could grab a bite before we left to go hiking," answered Joanna. "Someone downstairs could have heard me moving around above them; or someone could have seen me walking over to Glyn's flat, but I didn't notice them."

"So you have no checkable alibi for that morning and noon time." Owain gave a long sigh and leaned over to kiss Joanna. "Let's call it a night, shall we?"

"Just a minute, someone downstairs could have heard me moving around above them; or someone could have seen me walking over to Glyn's flat, but I didn't notice them." Joanna claimed.

XI

A n d e r s o n ' s   J o u r n a l

Owain reached McDowell in his room at the hotel early the next morning.

"I want to give you important information that has just been passed on to me. It seems that Anderson kept a journal. Look for the journal in his locker or desk at the lab he shared with two other geologists at the university. It may have evidence showing that Glyn was emotionally unbalanced. His love of protecting the environment may have unsettled him mentally. From what I understand, he wrote his experiments in his journal, but also his personal thoughts. Shedweld's name may appear there along with negative opinions or comments about him. This could help to confirm Joanna's statement concerning his reasons for suicide, and may answer why there wasn't a suicide note at his flat.

"The journal may have enough information to confirm his hatred of Shedweld, and there may be something about Sutter's death as well. I remember something that he said to me using the words *Mother Earth*. Check with the people who live around Glyn's flat again. Did he go out early in the morning in his car, and then came back before noon in his car? There has to be someone who spotted him. Also check with the couple who live downstairs from Joanna's friend, where she was staying. Hopefully, they would have heard Joanna moving around up in the flat during the time of Shedweld's murder that morning."

Sgt. McDowell told Owain about the charts that Supt. Jones had set up for the teams of detectives to use for their investigative work and mentioned that Lady Joanna Whitecoft was the only suspect listed for the murders of Shedweld and Anderson.

Owain was deeply disturbed by this news; he knew the press would spin the story in all the papers. He asked McDowell if Jones was going to court for a warrant for Joanna's arrest.

"The big block to that is the motive problem, sir. She has no clear motive for killing Shedweld or Anderson. The judge will recognized this fact. This is my opinion, of course."

"McDowell, find other suspects and delay Jones from arresting her as long as you can. If you find the journals and there is material in them that we can use, we have a chance to make a case either for suicide or for a new suspect in the murder of Shedweld. You can reach me on my cell phone. Good luck," said Owain.

Owain went down to breakfast. As he passed her bedroom door he noticed that the room was empty. He hoped everyone had slept soundly last night. His uncle's room was not far from his, and Catherine's was just down the hall. As Owain entered, they were both enjoying breakfast in the sunny morning room. Joanna was in the big old kitchen making scrambled eggs, toast, and ham.

"Good morning, Owain, you slept in, I guess? Joanna has cooked a wonderful breakfast. She has been down here waiting on us," said Uncle Hywel with a laugh.

Joanna walked in with two plates of breakfast for Owain and herself. Aunt Catherine poured coffee into his cup and passed the milk. Uncle Hywel sat smiling from ear to ear. "Nothing like having the aristocrats to wait upon you . . . what?" joked Uncle Hywel.

Back at their hotel, near police headquarters in Wales, McDowell and Landers ate breakfast, then rushed over to Prof. Anderson's lab office at university to check on locating his journal. As they entered the lab, Edward and Brian looked up. They recognized McDowell immediately when he and Anderson were at the cave while the dig was going on. It was also the day that Anderson had his fit of rage about someone digging up gold and other artifacts.

"We would like to search Dr. Anderson's desk and locker." Landers showed his Scotland Yard ID."

"Where is chief inspector Wallon? We thought he would be with you." Said Edward who was part of Prof. Anderson's team, both of them were in shock over Glyn's death.

McDowell said, "We are here on a criminal investigation into the death of Dr. Anderson, and want to look through his possessions."

"I see, of course, his desk is here, and his locker is over there next to other lockers. I will show you which one is Glyn's."

McDowell walked to the locker and Landers searched through the desk. On the top shelf of the locker under some file folders was an ordinary journal. McDowell removed it from the locker and put it into his evidence bag. Landers was busy going through the things in the desk. He asked one of the geologists if they had a box into which they might put the items from the desk. McDowell went through the rest of the locker contents. Landers questioned the two men about the last time that they had seen or spoken with Dr. Anderson, then McDowell and Landers left with the boxes after thanking Edward and Brian the two close friends of Anderson's for their help.

"Now," Inspector Landers said. "We must go back to headquarters to investigate what we have found. I'm sure those friends of Anderson will be calling Jones's office about our visit."

Landers was right. Jones was waiting for them when they entered district headquarters. "You didn't inform me that you were going to the university labs."

"Well, sir, we received a tip, and we thought that we should act upon it right away. These items may hold important evidence concerning this case. We didn't want anyone tampering with evidence in the lab desk and locker before we could search them," explained McDowell. He watched Jones for any reactions.

"I see, McDowell—and what have you got there?"

"Journal, sir" McDowell was busy looking for the name Shedweld, and also an emotional note that could confirm that Anderson was contemplating committing suicide. He found both. As the others listened, he read from the journal's notes concerning Shedweld. The comment in the journal had been written by Anderson after he had ranted and raved to the others in the cave about the desecration of the little gold vein. McDowell continued to read from Anderson's journal as he rambled on about Mother Earth and mentioned that he had avenged her. There is more: Anderson refers to his little pistol as "the avenger." They are all shocked to find this new information and realize that Jones was going down the wrong line of inquiry into the murder and suicide.

Inspector Landers spoke up, suggesting that the journal be sent to Scotland Yard labs in London for handwriting analysis. A psychologist should be called in to analyze the content of the more personal writings in the journal for evidence of Anderson's mental stability.

"Well, until we have reports on the analyses, we will not arrest Lady Joanna Whitecoft. If Professor Anderson killed Dirk Otis Shedweld, it will make our investigation less complicated." Landers and McDowell looked at each other and immediately made arrangements for the journal and the box of other items to be taken from the lab and sent by courier to Scotland Yard Special Branch labs. They were pleased with the result of their investigation. Perhaps now Jones would not be in such a rush to push for a warrant for Lady Joanna's arrest for murder.

The other shoe was about to drop. In a newspaper, the story on the newsstands the headlines read:

"Lady Joanna Whitecoft, daughter of Lord Peter Whitecoft, is accused of murdering two men. Dirk Otis Shedweld, a prominent businessman of England and Australia, was shot by Lady Joanna while he attempted to enter his car at his cottage. She then returned to the flat of a prominent environmentalist, Professor Glyn Anderson, a world famous geologist, and gruesomely shot him in the head over a lover's quarrel. Her murder spree may have started with another famous geologist's murder, Dr. Sutter. This devilish woman's exploits are being covered up by one of Scotland Yard's gay blades, Chief Inspector Owain Wallon. They have been seen together gadding about at one of London's finest French restaurants. Lady Whitecoft and Chief Inspector Wallon made no secret of their intimate relationship. But then! This very dapper young beau of Lady Whitecoft's has the looks of one of England's finest ducal families. Obviously, he is a descendent of another romantic escapade many years ago which transpired, and produced one of the noble families' many illegitimate offspring, during a romantic weekend at the duke's estate." The byline was none other than Du-vrey's reporter friend, Bert Dagart.

The scandal sheets ate up the story. The paparazzi were on the scent along with photographers falling all over each other, trying to locate the murderess and her partner, Chief Inspector Wallon. Sir Gordon sat at his desk, ready to murder the press himself. Lord Peter Whitecoft headed for his country estate, knowing that the press was at his heels. McDowell, Landers, and Supt. Jones read the news release in utter disbelief. McDowell ran to the telephone to make sure that the courier with the vital evidence had not been waylaid by scandal-seeking reporters.

Owain and Joanna were spending a relaxing afternoon in Aunt Catherine's rose garden when the telephone rang. Owain knew both Aunt Catherine and Uncle Hywel would sometimes take naps in the afternoon. He picked up the phone and heard Tom's excited voice on the other end. Owain listened in horror as Tom read to him just one of the articles from the rag sheets.

"Don't go anywhere; stay indoors, and away from windows. It is just a matter of time before they find out where you are. Right now, I have been told that the reporters, with Bert Dagart egging them on, are scouring the Snowdonia area trying to find you. They are also around here at The Ormes Victoria Hotel. The reporters are hounding the district police station as well. You had best talk with your aunt and uncle. These reporters can be mean and rude when they are on the prowl for a story," added Tom.

Owain thanked Tom for warning him. He went outside and found Joanna taking a snooze in the garden on a chaise lounge.

As Owain approached, Joanna woke up. "We have to go inside. There is trouble," he told her.

"What has happened?"

Owain related what Tom had told him about the newspaper articles and the reporters hunting for them.

"*Am I being arrested?*" asked Joanna with a worried look on her face.

"I don't know. McDowell hasn't called. We have to wait for his phone call. If it is the worst, we will see a police car arriving soon. Right now, I am more concerned about the reporters banging on the doors of Gorwyn Hall with their cameras flashing. Go upstairs and wait for me to call you. I am going to try and reach McDowell."

Catherine came down the stairs as Joanna was going up. "What is going on?" she asked.

Hywel appeared on the balcony above and asked the same question. Owain suggested that they come into Uncle Hywel's library. He checked outside for any sign of cars arriving. Then Owain explained what had happened: the stories in the newspapers and persistent reporters chasing around trying to find out where Joanna and he were located.

Finally, the telephone rang again. Owain asked his uncle to answer it, but to say nothing to anyone about where he and Joanna were. Hywel answered the telephone and turned to Owain.

"Your Sergeant McDowell is calling. Do you want to talk with him?"

"Yes." Owain took the receiver from his uncle's extended hand. "Sergeant?"

"Yes, sir, it is McDowell here. Have you seen the newspapers?"

"No, Tom called and read the articles to me."

"Don't worry, sir, we have Professor Anderson's journal. This is a very important piece of evidence that has been sent to our labs in London to be verified. The journal mentions Shedweld and many other things. Superintendent Jones is not arresting Lady Joanna. The journal gives evidence of Anderson's state of mind, too. It looks like he might have killed Shedweld and then committed suicide. This news story does not have the recently found facts from the journal. It was put out before we found the journal. However, the newspaper hounds don't know that, and they are still on your trail. You had best stay out of sight until this matter can be cleared up, sir."

"Fine, we will do that. Thanks for all you have done. Will turn on my cell phone, and you can reach me that way. I forgot that I had turned it off when I went to bed last night."

Owain turned to discuss the situation with his aunt and uncle. On the television, the news commentator was just giving the details about the murders and Joanna's involvement by quoting from the articles in the papers.

"Those blasted media hounds! They destroy people's privacy for the sake of news stories," said Uncle Hywel angrily. His sister stood next to him with a disturbed and anxious look on her face. She had grasped the reference in the article about Owain's parentage, and the disclosure about Owain's birth identity. In the past it had been convenient to ignore this topic. Now the press, in one swift blow, had brought up the past, and she must face it. Owain at this point had overlooked this disclosure about him in the newspapers. His immediate concern was for Joanna.

In London, a press office of scandal seekers, including Dagart, were searching for a lead to find the location of Lady Joanna Whitecoft and her lover. They had stumbled on information given them by an outside gossip seeker disclosing Owain Wallon's background. The real interest for their story was locating Lady Joanna Whitecoft, the murderess.

"We must have overlooked a location where Joanna Whitecoft could have gone for privacy. The police are not going to reveal anything to us. They may have sequestered her in a holding area."

"I don't think so. She is probably hidden with friends."

"We have spoken to her closest friends. They are just as perturbed as we are about the fact that she murdered Glyn Anderson. I think that they would tell us where she is, if they knew. No, it has to be with someone else that we have overlooked," speculated one of the reporters.

"Reporters have checked Chief Inspector Owain Wallon's flat, and talked with the neighbors," said another reporter.

"*OWAIN—that's it. He is from Wales. But where in Wales?* I am going to do some digging. They won't help me at the Yard. I know. I remember reading something about a Wallon who was promoted at the Yard's Special Branch. There it is. He came from Wales and grew up at a place called Gorwyn Hall," said another reporter.

Using his computer, the reporter tracked down Gorwyn Hall's location on the map. "Yes! Yes! That's it. Get the word out to meet us at Gorwyn Hall," said Bert Dagart.

Back at Gorwyn Hall, enjoying supper and a glass of wine, Owain and the others heard the sound of car tires as they squealed up the gravel driveway. The press had found them. Hywel hurried to the telephone to call the police in town. Catherine and Joanna headed for the upstairs rooms. Owain went for the front entry. He could hear the reporters pounding on the heavy front doors all the way through to the back of the house. Reaching the doors, He carefully opened them and stepped outside with his badge in hand to face the crowd of reporters.

Over the din of their questions, Owain told them to leave. They were trespassing on private property. After making that statement, he reentered the entrance hall, and met Uncle Hywel as he returned from calling the police. They could hear the reporters at the back door, and some were looking in the windows. Camera flashes were going off, while reporter's feet trashed the bushes at some of the windows. Soon the sirens of the local constable and police could be heard as they answered Hywel's urgent call for help. Constable Davis ordered the reporters to leave immediately. After the police moved towards them, the reporters left, and went directly to the local pub for tidbits of information for their stories. The locals felt that they were being invaded. However, some of the locals jumped at the chance to talk to the press. All this attention had gone to their heads. When Hywel later heard about their gabbing tongues, he went down to the pub and gave them a verbal thrashing in Welsh.

Back at Gorwyn Hall, the sheep herdsmen who worked for Catherine offered their help. Elena and her daughter Agnes came up to stay again. Agnes was very upset and said she would feel safer staying in her bedroom. Aunt Catherine understood about Agnes; she was mentally retarded, and the commotion made her very nervous.

Aunt Catherine returned upstairs after the police left. She had gone to a cabinet in her sitting room of off bedroom where she kept family papers and photographs. Opening one of the glass doors, she reached in and removed three bundles of letters carefully tied with pink satin ribbon. One bundle at a time, she unwrapped the pink ribbon around them. She reached for the first letter in the nearest bundle. Unfolding the letter and smoothing out the old stationary, she started to read. Soon tears came to her eyes, and she laid down the letter on the desks.

Hearing a knock, she went to her door to find Hywel standing there. "I thought that I would find you here. I see that you have taken out Elizabeth's letters. May I come in and sit with you for awhile?" Hywel said in a stressed voice.

"Yes, of course you can, Hywel." He took the easy chair next to her desk.

"What do you plan to do with the letters? Show them to Owain?"

"I was sitting here looking at the first one, and I started to cry. How can I explain to Owain about his mother and her sad marriage? She was such a lovely girl, and Edward Wallon was so arrogant. He loved fast cars, sailing, and tennis. He showed very little affection for her, and their son. The night before the accident, he was out partying with his friends. They all thought of Elizabeth as that Welsh farmer's daughter who was not from their class."

"Now, Catherine, let's not dredge up the past. Owain needn't read those letters. I would burn them if I were you. All we need to tell him are the facts of his father's birth. Edward Wallon was raised by the duke's family governess, who was about to retire. The duke gave her a cottage and a nice pension. He added an allowance for the child who, Mary Wallon had agreed to bring up. She was not to mention the natural mother's name, because she had been the duke's house guest, and there would be a scandal. Since the governess's name was Mary Wallon, he asked that the boy be called Edward Wallon. A story could be put forth that Edward was her nephew, and his parents had been killed in India. Since everyone knew that Mary Wallon had a brother who had been killed in India, the story would sound reasonable. Mary had lived on the duke's estate for many years after graduating from university. She was a very well educated woman who had come from a fine family. The family had gone on hard times. She spoiled the boy, and he grew up with little regard for responsibility," said Hywel.

Catherine had pulled out photographs of their sister Elizabeth with Edward shortly after their wedding. There were more photographs of the couple standing next to Edward's sport car. Elizabeth was holding a baby in her arms. Also there was a picture of Owain, holding his favorite teddy bear. The teddy bear burned in the car crash that had killed Owain's parents. Somehow, Owain was thrown clear and only slightly hurt. He had been five years old at the time.

Hywel sighed and Catherine picked up the letters and took his suggestion. She threw them into the fireplace. The dried stationary soon went up in flames and burned away. Hywel suggested that they go downstairs and have a cup of tea.

XII

Family Secret Disclosed

Days later, the facts and additional information started to surface. Both McDowell and Landers, through diligent detective work, had turned up new evidence in three murder cases—Sutter's bludgeoning on the hiking trail, Shedweld shot from the back, and Anderson's death by a bullet to the head. The third case was officially being considered a murder rather than a self-inflicted death, but was being carefully reexamined for any new information.

The labs at Scotland Yard had confirmed the authenticity of the journal found in Anderson's locker at the university. After reviewing the statements of Anderson's colleagues, new information was coming out with details of the last days of the professor's life.

He had shown signs of being seriously agitated and stressed. In his medical files, they found evidence of another emotional breakdown in the past, during a period when he had become violent. It could be proved that this recent attack led him to commit two murders. The first, it was thought, was Ted Sutter on the hiking trail. He and Ted got into a fight over mining for gold in Snowdonia. Anderson was against mining altogether in Wales, and especially for gold. The argument led to his losing control and striking out at Ted Sutter—he hit him over the head with his sturdy hiking stick. With this new possibility in mind, McDowell and Landers went back to Glyn Anderson's flat. They located the hiking stick with hair and dried blood on the knob. The solid, sturdy stick was sent out for lab tests, and the hair and blood samples matched samples taken from Ted Sutter's body. A match for Anderson's fingerprints was taken from the handle of the stick.

Apparently, Anderson had become enraged when he realized that Shedweld was going to steal gold from Welsh mines and trick investors into giving money for an invented "large mining operation" in Australia.

The developing scenario indicated that Professor Glyn Anderson had gone to Shedweld to tell him off and make it clear to him that he would not allow him to destroy anymore of Snowdonia's environment. Shedweld probably laughed at him, and perhaps even threatened to have the professor killed if he tried to stop the mining operation by notifying the authorities in Great Britain. This second explosion of rage on Anderson's part moved him to return to his car, pull out his pistol, and shoot Shedweld in the back as he stood next to his car at the cottage. After returning to his flat, Anderson's mind cracked. He could not think of living any longer with the realization that he had to kill to protect "Mother Nature."

After he had returned from Shedweld's and was about to commit suicide, Joanna entered his flat. Anderson knew that she would convince him to not go through with it. He couldn't allow that to happen. He was too far over the edge—he had not the will left to go on with his life, speculated the two detectives.

The pistol from that morning's killing was on the desk in front of him. He grabbed it and shot himself. At that very moment, as Joanna entered the flat she ran forward and reached for the pistol. As Anderson fell she grabbed the pistol from him, but it had already gone off. They both fell to the floor, and she was left grabbing at the barrel of the gun in one hand, and with the other hand pulled his bleeding head into her lap. The constable entered from up the street after everyone heard the gun shot. The constable gave testimony that he saw Joanna holding onto the barrel of the gun. He saw Anderson on the floor next to Joanna with his head in her lap. She couldn't have fired the gun. Her finger prints were on the barrel of the gun only. Professor Anderson's prints were on the trigger and handle. However, Jones' investigation fails to establish this important fact. Both McDowell and Landers could not understand why the fingerprints discrepancy was not noted. Was it just faulty police investigation or an oversight?

When another witness report was made to the police, they failed to review what this witness had said. While the woman was walking on the street that same morning, before the shooting occurred, she looked up at the window of the building where Joanna was staying and saw her sitting there while writing her report about the previous evening's meeting. Also the people downstairs had heard Joanna moving around upstairs in her friend's flat that morning. Joanna was therefore absolved from any involvement in the murder of Shedweld. The police looked at these witnesses' previous statements again more carefully.

The first murder of the workman at the docks was carried out by Denton and Older under the orders of Shedweld. Also brought out was the dynamiting of the hill above Owain's car accident. That was done by Sutter and Denton. Owain's car was not the target. It was merely in the wrong place at the wrong time.

The financial scheme constructed by Shedweld had illegally collected a large amount of investors' capital for his scheme. They were now searching for what happened to that capital. Further investigation into his business dealings showed that Shedweld was a big-time dealer in stolen artifacts as well. He was bartering deals in Australia and South America. Wales was a good location to lie low and not be observed. The geologist Sutter had convinced Shedweld that there was gold to be mined in Wales.

The memorial service for Anderson took place the next day. His ashes were to be spread over the mountains of Snowdonia. It was a beautiful sunny day as the grief-stricken group walked out to Glyn's favorite hiking trail. Owain and Joanna joined the others and watched two of Glyn's closest buddies,Edward and Brian leave the group. They carried the small packages of ashes they would spread over Glyn's adored countryside. After the memorial service, Owain and Joanna returned to Gorwyn Hall where Catherine and Hywel had been waiting for them.

During the last few days there hadn't been very much time for relaxing by any of them. The reporters had tried to keep the gossip story going, but with Joanna absolved of any murder charges, they were left with little to write about. Dagart had left his buddies with the task of filling in the voids on the gossip pages with another story.

Owain hoped that the press would leave them alone. The gossip item about his parentage was disturbing, and he was trying to find a way to approach his aunt without upsetting her too much.

Catherine was also in a dilemma as to how she was going to convey the information about his father's parentage to Owain. There was no use setting aside the sorrowful story any longer.

When Joanna and Owain returned from the memorial service they discovered on the large table in the drawing room, were three old photographs in beautiful sterling frames. Owain walked over and picked up the one showing the man and woman. Uncle Hywel approached him from behind.

"We haven't been totally forth coming concerning your parents. The woman in the photo is your mother, Elizabeth Gorwyn Wallon. The man standing next her is your father Edward Wentworth Wallon. They were married here at Gorwyn Hall two years before you were born." Uncle Hywel explained. Owain set the picture down and reached for the next photograph.

"That one is of the three of you shortly after you were born." Uncle Hywel said. "The last photograph is of you, just before your fifth birthday, holding onto your favorite teddy bear." Aunt Catherine had come to join them while they looked at the photographs.

Owain stood in front of the table, first picking up one beautifully framed photograph , looking down at the next one. Finally he picked up the third one and studied it carefully; the last one was of himself and his favorite toy.

"I remember that bear. What happened to it?"

Hywel replied. "When the sports car accident occurred you were saved but the Teddy bear was destroyed in the fire."

"I see. Who was Edward Wentworth Wallon?"Owain turned and asked both of them.

"Your father was the illegitimate son of a duke and one of the lady guests at one of the duke's weekend parties. She retired from society during the pregnancy, and gave birth to your father on her family's estate." Uncle Hywel explained all this simply.

"We think that when Edward was away at university, someone leaked the information of his illegitimate birth to him. His guardian, Mary Wallon, would not confirm what she called "wretched gossip." We never knew her, you see. She died before Edward married Elizabeth, my sister."

Aunt Catherine had returned to sitting at the far end of the drawing room in a corner with a handkerchief to her face. Joanna was also there, sitting in a chair gazing out the window. Uncle Hywel put his hand on Owain's shoulder.

"We have tried to make up for the loss of your parents, especially your mother. It has been such a pleasure having you grow up here with us at Gorwyn Hall; and we are so very proud of you. Knowing this does not change the fact that we are still your family, does it?" Uncle Hywel asked.

"No! of course not. As I told Joanna, I love you both very much. It's unfortunate that I had to find out about my father this way through the gossiping press. Sooner or later I know you would have told me. I'm sorry that you were forced to tell me under these circumstances. There is absolutely no interest on my part to locate records of my natural grandfather or grandmother. That occurred in the long-forgotten past. My grandparents did the right thing at the time. Otherwise my father might have been sent into a foster home without any name at all. As it turned out, he received loving care by his stepmother, Mary Wallon. If he turned out somewhat wild, it could not have been her fault," said Owain. "Maybe someday I will find a picture of Mary Wallon."

Hywel smiled and nodded; then he took out glasses and a bottle of wine.

"Well, let's have a toast to the future," Owain said. He raised his glass to his aunt and uncle. Joanna came over to join them and to give Owain a kiss. She was pretty sure she knew who his grandparents had been. There was a portrait in a famed gallery of a man he strongly resembled—but this was not the time to discuss the subject.

At the same time, returning to London from Sydney was Louis Duvrey. He had read the reports concerning the murders in Snowdonia and Joanna's involvement and had informed his friends that this was a dastardly deed to have killed his prominent friend Dirk Otis Shedweld. It was his plan to have the case reopened. He would find a way to avenge the murder of Dirk Otis Shedweld. He was not satisfied that Prof. Anderson had committed suicide after having killed his friend Ted Sutter. There was much more to this case, Duvrey thought. Besides, Lady Joanna was a thorn in Duvrey's side and he wouldn't mind seeing her hang for at least one of the murders.

His attitude concerning that lady ran deep. Some time ago she had rejected his romantic advances, and he never forgot this insult. HE, Duvrey, was a man of great pride, and they would find that he was also very cunning. He planned to contact his friend Burt Dagart again and set the attack on Joanna's innocence in motion.

All of his life Duvrey had felt cheated out of his true place in an aristocratic society that he felt owed him recognition. His connection to Shedweld was to bring him a fortune to invest in his dream of a wealthy lifestyle. However, he would soon realize that Shedweld had left him a connection to another in the world of corruption. Duvrey had attracted the interest of another leader who could use him. This evil man was far away. "A true *tai-pan* who was looking for the perfect English gentleman to carry out this warlord's revenge on his long held hate for the colonial British."

As Owain prepared to return to London, Chief Superintendent Gordon called, to tell Owain to prepare to leave for Australia. He was being sent to work with the Australian authorities on the investigation of the gold mine leases that Shedweld's firm claimed to own. The money of the investors had to be verified, and traced to the funds' improper use. Investors were seeking information into the large sum of money that had been allocated for the use of mining at these sites. Owain understood that the investigation was unfinished.

The Search for Stolen Funds

On the other side of the globe, Chief Inspector Owain Wallon was met at the airport in Sydney by Inspector Jed Hawkins. While they rode to headquarters, Inspector Hawkins commented, "You just missed your friend from the British foreign office, Louis Duvrey. He is returning to London and asked me to say 'hello' for him." Owain made a grimace, and replied that he was indeed acquainted with Duvrey. For a short time they both had worked for the Yard's Special Branch.

Upon reaching government offices, Wallon and Hawkins were escorted to a meeting room to find several agents from government financial affairs waiting for them. Owain shook their hands, and proceeded to open his briefcase to remove the files that Sir Gordon had briefed him on before he left London. During his long trip, Owain had had plenty of time to review and study the reports of the investments that the Shedweld's firm had been making. It was quite obvious that it would be necessary to verify the licenses for three very productive gold mines located in the back country of Australia.

After handing out copies of these reports to the others, Owain asked if they had found the licenses for the mining operations at these locations. A gentleman at the end of the table took a sip from his coffee mug and began.

"To the best of our knowledge, and after a thorough investigation by my staff, there are no such licenses or any such mine

locations. The gold mines in Australia are all very thoroughly documented by our agency, and there has not been any contract with
Mr. Shedweld's businesses with gold mining or the investment in
gold mining in this country. We are aware of his business activities,
and we can assure you that none of these businesses have illegal
activities in Australia. To our knowledge, none have been involved
with gold mining.

"This information that you bring comes as a complete surprise
to us. In the past, Mr. Shedweld's business has been very successful in metal salvaging work and other kinds of construction-based
projects. He seemed to manage a very legitimate business. We were
shocked to hear of his murder. From your reports, there are investors who have provided Mr. Shedweld with a sizable amount of
capital to be invested for them in gold mines located here in Australia. That just is not true. We have contacted the business office
of Mr. Shedweld, and they have denied ever having any knowledge
of such investments. If he has transferred large sums of money to
Australia, we should be able to trace it for you."

This came as no surprise to Owain. He was sure that Shedweld
had to have deposited the funds in a private offshore bank account.
But how could he find the account's location? As diplomatically as
possible, since Shedweld had been a respected citizen of Australia,
Owain had to find some way to recruit their help in talking with
people here in Australia without appearing overbearing—as the
British were often perceived.

Inspector Hawkins spoke up. "There may be a way that we can
aid Chief Inspector Wallon in this matter. Since Mr. Shedweld was
murdered in the UK, our investigation can become part of a criminal investigation. We can help the chief inspector by investigating
who might have some knowledge of the crime here in Australia."

The government official who had previously spoken said,
"From that perspective, I have no difficulty with the investigation;
and we should give the chief inspector our cooperation."

Hawkins escorted Owain to his office at police headquarters
where the two men discussed the criminal aspects of the case.
Owain was suffering seriously from jet lag and had trouble concen-
trating. Hawkins took pity on him once he realized this and drove
Owain to his hotel to check in. They agreed to meet for dinner that

night. Hawkins hoped that by that time, he would have information for him after speaking with people involved with Shedweld's
business activities.

Owain and Inspector Hawkins met in the hotel dining room
for dinner. Owain wanted to know what Jed had discovered.

"This case you have brought to our attention is tricky. The best
way to find the information you are looking for is not through regular channels. I called up a buddy of mine in the Bureau of Mine
Licenses for recent gold mine information. Evidently, someone
else had checked about applying for a license. After receiving a
copy of the necessary forms sent to them, the license bureau never
heard from this person again. The inquiry came from someone in
England. After that I spoke to a friend of mine who knows people
in the British Foreign Office here in Sydney. They told me that
Louis Duvrey had very good connections with various government
people. The other comment was not very complimentary: He was
a stuffed shirt. Most people avoided him. I was able to get a list of
the contacts in Australia who were wined and dined by Duvrey fre-
quently. Mostly, they are wealthy businessmen. I also found out that
Duvrey let everyone know that he was a very close friend of Lord
Peter Whitecoft and was engaged to his daughter."

Upon hearing that little bit of news, Owain raised his eyebrows
and grinned. He was sure that he had found the base of operations
for Duvrey's and Shedweld's financial scheme. Duvrey knew a way
to transfer funds to Australia very conveniently. How much could
he trust Jed Hawkins, who was giving him the information? Owain
wondered.

Hawkins must have read Owain's mind. He handed across the
table his official government identity card. Like Owain, Jed was in
a special branch of the government that was investigating financial
fraud.

"We have been in conversation with Sir Gordon at Scotland
Yard. Since this case involves people from the Foreign Office of
Great Britain as well as government officials and business men in
Australia, we must be very careful in our investigation. Dirk Otis
Shedweld's remains are to be returned to Sydney shortly. A large
funeral is planned that will include many well-known people. It
would be best if you were not seen at the funeral. Someone may

recognize you. We have men attending who will take pictures of everyone in attendance. The photographs will be made available to you. Also, our connections believe that you yourself may be in some danger. Shedweld was known to have kept armed guards, and to use them to silence people. So far, we have been unable to pin any of the killings on him. We have information from an informer that Duvrey has made use of these armed guards on at least one occasion. Again, evidence could not be found to establish Duvrey as an accessory to murder. So I advise you to be careful. Staying at this hotel is a very good idea. You are safer here than at a more economical place. I think your superior knew what he was doing when he made these arrangements."

"Mm—this presents a problem for me as to what I can accomplish here. I am hoping that you can provide me with more information on the contacts that Shedweld used to move funds to safe havens," said Owain.

"Have patience, we are working on it right now. The business records at his office here were not helpful. We could get a warrant to search his house. The judge would want probable cause for such a warrant; and since the funeral arrangements are underway, we would have a difficult time persuading a judge to give us the warrant. Because of Shedweld's close ties with important people in this country, we must move with caution."

At that moment, Hawkins's cell phone buzzed. "Excuse me for a minute." A moment later, a seriously disturbed look came over the man's face. "We must return to headquarters quickly!" he said.

Owain grabbed his briefcase and they left the restaurant. Back in Hawkins's office, Owain poured himself and Jed a cup of coffee, while the inspector talked on the phone. Two other inspectors came in and sat down.

Hawkins hung up. "There is word from London," he said. "Lord Peter Whitecoft's estate is in receivership by a financial broker claiming that Lord Whitecoft used his estate as collateral on a loan to buy a gold mine in Australia. This financial broker is representing a bank in Perth. As we have already been told, there are no gold mines on record that Lord Whitecoft could have bought. The funds for the purchase of the gold mine have been withdrawn from the business account with this bank. The Family Bank of Perth has closed on his loan, and requested repayment. Lord Whitecoft is unable to raise the funds."

How can this bank in Perth foreclose on a loan when there is no gold mine on record in Australia to back up their claim on Lord Whitecofts loan foreclosure?" asked Wallon.

"I am sorry. I can't answer that question. But there is more happening to the Whitecoft family," said Inspector Hawkins.

"I am sorry to report there is further bad news concerning the Whitecoft family's daughter, Joanna Whitecoft. She has been arrested and charged with the murder of Dirk Otis Shedweld. The case has been reopened on new evidence. She is being held in north Wales Police Headquarters. Also, a famous hotel in North Wales called the Ormes Victoria has had a serious fire. Lady Joanna was arrested while staying at this hotel as a guest of Mr. Tom Lewis, the manager," added Inspector Jed Hawkins. "They believe the fire was deliberately set to allow Miss Whitecoft to attempt an escape. The local police are investigating."

Owain's face went white as a sheet upon hearing this news. Taking a minute to collect his thoughts, he then asked to use the telephone to call Sir Gordon and request permission to return to London immediately. The home office put him through to Sir Gordon's private line.

Superintendent Gordon was very understanding, but refused Owain's request to return to London. Instead he told Owain to continue his investigation into the details of the financial scheme, and to acquire more details on the transactions between the bank in Perth and Shedweld. Sir Gordon indicated that at this time, Wallon could do best by all involved by investigating this bank.

Torn by not being able to return to Wales immediately to aid Joanna, and the instructions of Sir Gordon to continue his assignment in Australia, Owain was angry. For the first time, personal concerns had put a demand on his responsibilities as a police officer. Owain turned towards Hawkins and the other two officers with a stern look on his face.

"We must achieve results in this case soon. Hawkins, can your people investigate this bank in Perth? We need to know what the connection is with Shedweld, because I am sure that there is one. Who are the others involved with this financial scheme to defraud investors? Who else has invested with them and lost large sums of money?" Owain fought to contain his emotions.

"The gentleman at the head of the table who answered your questions about mine licensing is one of our suspects in this case. You can see that this investigation is very sensitive. We have felt for a long time that we have some idea of who is involved. No matter how hard we try, we have not been able to crack it open. Investigators are in sensitive places, attempting to locate evidence to bring these people to trial for financial fraud. By making a move such as this one on Lord Peter Whitecoft, it would appear that they are intent on scaring any of the investors from coming forward with evidence," said Inspector Hawkins.

"May I use your phone again? I want to contact my sergeant back in Wales."

"Certainly—go right ahead." The others left the office while Owain made his call.

"McDowell, is that you?"

"Yes, sir I guess you have heard the sad news about Lady Joanna being arrested."

"Please explain to me how this could have happened," said Owain in disbelief.

"As you heard, the murder case of Shedweld has been reopened. A person in the village of Dewi Sant claimed that he saw Lady Whitecoft drive up to Shedweld's cottage the morning of the murder. She was alone and in Glyn Anderson's car. Shortly afterward, she was seen returning at high speed down the driveway, and drove away. The witness had forgotten at first about seeing her, but felt later that it was important. Since the police claimed that the murder weapon was the same as the one found after Anderson committed suicide, it made Lady Whitecoft a murder suspect again. Even with the comments in Anderson's journal, there was not conclusive proof that he murdered Shedweld. Lady Whitecoft had a sounder motive. If she knew her father was in serious debt."

"Tell me, McDowell, is there a ballistics report on both bullets to substantiate that they both came from the same pistol found in Glyn's flat?"

"You know, sir, I don't know, but I will check on that right away, and get back to you."

"Who do they suspect set the fire at The Ormes Victoria Hotel?"

"The police believe Lady Whitecoft did it to divert being captured and arrested by the police. You do know that she is the same person who locked us in the cave—you, Jones, Anderson, and me. That little lady is in a pack of trouble," McDowell told Owain.

"Oh, blast! Get back to me as soon as you can."

Owain hung up and ran his fingers through his hair. He slammed his fist down on the desk in front of him, sending his coffee mug to the floor. Jed Hawkins returned to his office.

"You look wrung out—and you're clearly upset. But I think we have made a breakthrough. There is a bank in Perth, unbeknownst to us, which was recently sold to Shedweld when the president of the bank died. If we can prove that Shedweld has been using the bank as a cover for his fraudulent business transactions, we can charge his own bank with fraud. First thing in the morning, we will take a flight to Perth and go over their books. Right now, tonight, there is not very much we can do. I suggest that you return to your hotel and get a good night's rest. I will have one of my officers drive you there."

Inspector Hawkins looked over at Wallon and realized that this case was taking a nasty turn. Owain picked up his briefcase and left.

Back at the hotel, in his room, he called Tom Lewis, who, McDowell had told him, was staying at Gorwyn Hall with Gwyneth.

"When are you returning? Everything is a mess here: first, the arrest of Joanna, and then the fire at the hotel."

"I heard that Joanna was supposed to have started the fire as a divergence."

"No, no, you heard wrong. Everything happened so close together that the police drew that conclusion. She didn't start the fire; she was staying with us at the cottage. Joanna was nowhere near where the fire started. The front desk called the cottage to tell us that the police were there with a warrant for Joanna's arrest. Joanna panicked and ran out the door. The police caught her as she ran down to the beach, handcuffed her, and took her back to police headquarters. The fire engines arrived and I spent the night seeing to the guests and the smoke damage to the building. The fire started in the kitchen. We have had to close the hotel because of the smoke damage. There was some structural damage as well, but reconstruction is underway.

"The newspapers, including our favorite gossip reporter, Dagart, made it sound like the hotel was almost completely destroyed and that Joanna had started the fire. Dagart was the one who tracked down and brought in the witness who claims to have seen Joanna at the cottage the morning Shedweld was murdered. Joanna is in a cell at the station. Only her lawyer and her father can see her. The trial is set for next month. Superintendent Jones is confident that she is guilty. McDowell is still around, but is pretty well blocked out. The local police headquarters and Jones as the acting superintendent has taken over the sole responsibility for investigating the case. Inspector Landers has returned to London. From what I have heard, Shedweld's body is to be returned to Sydney fairly soon to be buried there." Tom told Owain.

Owain said: "Sir Gordon insists that I must stay here in Sydney to investigate this financial fraud business. Tomorrow morning, I am to fly down with Inspector Hawkins to Perth. There is a small bank there that was bought by Shedweld and used by him to hide his ill-gotten funds from investors. If this proves to be true, then we can start to clear up and expose his scheme. Have you seen anything of Duvrey? He was supposed to have returned to England." Owain struggled to stay calm and think of ways to help Joanna.

"No, I haven't, but that doesn't mean that he is not here," responded Tom, who realized that his buddy in Australia must be driven to distraction.

"All right! McDowell is checking for me about the ballistics test on the two bullets that are supposed to have come from the pistol that was used to kill Shedweld and Anderson."

Tom told Owain that he would look into things, and call back as soon as possible. Meantime, McDowell was trying to reach Owain. He had some very interesting news.

"Sir, Jones and his officers are not cooperating with me. However, I threatened them in as pleasant a way as possible by telling them that they could be held responsible for withholding evidence from the defense. That got their attention, and they turned over the reports that I wanted.

"There were no ballistics tests done on the two bullets as they claimed since it seemed obvious that the two bullets had come from the same gun. The pistol at Anderson's flat when examined had two empty cartridges, and had been fired recently. I asked them to show me the two bullets. The answer was even stranger. They had only one of the bullets, the one from Anderson's head wound. The bullet from Shedwelds body could not be found. This was the reason that they gave me.

"On the day of the two murders, they were very short-handed. Ex-superintendent Cadwell had disappeared. The Shedweld body had been brought into the morgue by another district's team that had been helping out Jones's team. The follow-up team that had been organized under the supervision of the recently promoted Superintendent Jones assumed that the bullet from Shedweld's body had been properly examined and then stored with the rest of the evidence in the evidence room. The forensic people don't remember seeing the bullets; and it may still be in his body, which is on its way to Sydney. We know that the security room was the same area where the artifacts had been stolen. That evidence room secure storage area is a joke. They have serious problems at this police headquarters that is under investigation. " Sgt. McDowell relaid to Owain.

"Well, well, how very interesting. What does Joanna's lawyer have to say?"

"Townsend believes that the missing bullet puts doubt to a conviction in this case. We are also looking into the witness's story, which is very sketchy. It seems he stayed very late at the village pub and left there not too sober. He says that he was walking his dog when he saw Joanna in the car that drove up to Shedweld's cottage in the morning of the murder. The pub bartender doesn't believe he could have been sober enough to have been walking his dog at that time in the morning. No one else can vouch for seeing him walking his dog that morning. Obviously, his story is weak, sir," said McDowell. "However, I do remember that a witness claimed that he saw a car coming down the driveway but could not identify the man driving. I will check that out."

"Good job, McDowell. What is Jones's reason for his continuing attempt to find Joanna guilty of murder? He shouldn't care.

If Anderson killed Shedweld, as we all concluded, that should be enough," said Owain.

It was a nasty business, certainly. Owain hated to think that Glyn had done it. However, if he had gone berserk, then probably it had happened that way. This missing bullet was disturbing. The incompetence was amazing. *If the bullet from Shedweld's body had not come from Glyn's pistol, then whose?* He thought.

XIV

Perth Bank in Australia Searched

Very early in the morning, Inspector Hawkins had arranged tickets for a nonstop flight from Sydney Airport to Perth. The flight should take them about four hours, and they would land before lunch time. If they proceed directly to the Perth bank recently acquired by Shedweld's firm, there should be enough time to investigate the records and return to Sydney late the same day. It didn't leave very much time to go over records; but it would be enough, Hawkins thought, to enable them to apply for a warrant to locate the funds and prevent any transfer. These people of Shedweld's were moving pretty fast if they had started a foreclosure on property in England.

As their plane approached the city, Owain could make out the harbor. He was impressed by the number of large schooners and yachts moored there. After exiting the plane, Hawkins and Wallon made their way through the Perth airport terminal. They took a cab to the bank. Hawkins and Wallon observed from the car's windows that police cars and fire trucks had surrounded the bank building and neighboring structures.

The two officers jumped out before the cab had come to a full stop, leaving the cab. They rushed the rest of the way on foot. As they approached the police and fire trucks, the commander-in-charge of the fire trucks came forward and Hawkins showed his badge. The captain explained that a large explosion had occurred inside the Family Bank of Perth. The main vault door had been blown open and the vault robbed. Inspector Hawkins spoke to a

Perth police sergeant to get more information about the robbery and was told that no one had been hurt. As the explosion and robbery happened early in the morning, the employees had not been in the bank at the time.

The bank manager stepped over to the three men. "I am so sorry you had to come all this way. He said as he addressed Hawkins. "We could not reach you at your office. They told us that you had already left for Perth."

"Is your office still available? We need to speak with you about the contents of the vault," Hawkins said.

"Why yes, my office has not been destroyed. It is a mess, though." The bank manager showed concern on his face as again as he looked over at Chief Inspector Wallon.

"Then, we will follow you," Hawkins said.

The manager led Hawkins and Wallon into what had been his office. Owain left them to take a look around the damaged vault and to check on what was left of the inside. He then rejoined the others in the manager's office.

"Have you a record of the contents of the vault, and the amount of money that was there?" Wallon asked. Again the manager looked over at Wallon. Owain realized the manager did not know who he was, "I am Chief Inspector Wallon from Scotland Yard on a special mission to Sidney."

"I am pleased to meet you. About the records, I am afraid not. My computer was stolen by the thieves, and the paperwork was destroyed. I can give you a rough estimate; but until we contact all our customers, we can't have a complete accounting."

"What is your rough estimate?" Owain asked with growing impatience. Again the bank manager stared at Chief Inspector Wallon.

"Oh, I would guess somewhere in the neighborhood of several thousand dollars. We mostly have working-class customers and elderly pensioners. The teller cash boxes were not in the vault, but locked in the tellers drawers. We had some bonds and safety deposit boxes." Abruptly he changed the subject. "Why is a chief inspector from Scotland Yard Special Branch here?" The bank manager asked Inspector Hawkins. The manager's manner had become decidedly nervous and uncooperative.

Hawkins and Owain were stunned by the lack of information and competence displayed by the manager. They were sure he was lying concerning the amount of funds stolen. Shedweld must have used this bank to launder his funds. Why else would he buy a bank in Perth? There was no reason to continue talking to the manager. He was being uncooperative and this matter would have to include the Perth Police immediately Inspector Hawkins made a note to look into this bank manager's background. They left for Perth Police Headquarters.

Again there was not very much information about Shedweld and this bank that they could put in their reports until they could gather more facts. With the records destroyed in the explosion, it would take bank examiners weeks to put them in order. Also there were unanswered questions about how the robbers entered the bank before it was due to open. Someone let them in and the manager looks like he was involved.

At Police Headquarters, Hawkins and Wallon were given a piece of information from the local police that turned out to be very important. Shedweld owned his own dock at a marina in Fremantle harbor. He kept an ocean-equipped large yacht with a crew of three always available. The funds which Wallon and Hawkins were seeking could be leaving the country on Shedwelds yacht. Immediately, Owain and Hawkins called the marina in Fremantle. The manager at the marina office told them that Shedweld's yacht had left for Sydney. The yacht was to be moored in Sydney harbor before the funeral ceremony. Wallon and Hawkins worried that it was too late. They asked more questions, and were told that the yacht had been fueled to capacity and plenty of supplies brought on board. The harbor master had observed the vessel leaving the marina and heading north with a full crew and one passenger on board. The harbor master presumed that they would be heading out for the harbor in Sydney.

Hawkins looked at Wallon for suggestions. Going west and north was the long way around to reach Sidney. It was getting late. If they were to go after the yacht in a small plane it would have to be in the morning and it was too late to fly back to Sydney to night. He made a call to his superiors in Sydney, who gave him permission to procure a pilot and small plane to track the location of the yacht in the morning. If the yacht was in Australia's territorial waters he could contact the yacht captain through the pilot's radio and ask for their destination. There was nothing that they could do but stay the night in Fremantle. The Australian government authorities had been advised that this yacht could be carrying large sums of money stolen from a bank in Perth. There was a warrant issued for a search of the yacht when it arrived in Sidney. Wallon and Hawkins were not sure that yacht's real destination was Sydney but was heading for Indonesia or another safe harbor. There had to be someone else in charge of Shedweld's organization now that he was dead.

In the early morning the pilot headed the small Cessna up the coast towards the north.

"This is the long direction for a yacht to sail to Sydney," the pilot commented to the two passengers. Hawkins agreed with him.

The pilot soon announced that he had spotted the large yacht and would circle so they could contact the yacht captain and take pictures. Wallon was already at the window snapping pictures. Inspector Hawkins called to the yacht on the plane's radio and told them who he was. Suddenly from the deck of the yacht, their plane was fired upon. The pilot banked the Cessna and headed back towards Fremantle. He told them that being fired upon was not in his lease contract. One of the bullets had just missed hitting the plane's engine.

From the aircraft, Hawkins called his superiors about the yacht's location. He was told the bank manager had been taken into custody and questioned. After some bargaining went on, he told them that men from Shedweld's company had threatened him. They wanted the vault door opened. He told them that the door was on a time lock. They then blew open the vault door and went in to collect a large sum of money, bonds; even gold bars. The police did not believe his story. After more questioning he confessed to being a partner in one of Shedweld's companies. This did not surprise Wallon.

Hawkins said "If we hurry we will have just enough time to catch our plane back to Sydney." Obviously, Shedweld's yacht was heading for international waters which were out of their district of responsibility.

After landing in Sydney that night, Owain returned to his hotel. He put a call into Sir Gordon at Scotland Yard. Owain was satisfied that he had done all he could do on the financial end of the Shedweld case. Know it would be in the hands of international authorities. He was convinced that the funds were on that yacht.

Now, Joanna was his first concern, and he desperately wanted to return to help her any way he could. Townsend may have gotten her released from jail; however, that would not satisfy Owain until she was completely and finally absolved of the charge of murder. He wanted her name entirely cleared with no taint of committing any crime. Gordon might feel that there was a conflict of professional interests, but at this point Owain was ready to resign his position if necessary to keep her from being charged for a murder she did not commit.

The following morning, Owain reached Sir Gordon who complimented him on his investigation of Shedweld's financial affairs, and agreed that indeed he should return to London on the first available flight. Sergeant McDowell had sent him an extensive report concerning the Anderson and Shedweld murder cases. McDowell had explained to Sir Gordon about the follow-up he had done on Owain's questions concerning the bullets and the witnesses. Sir Gordon admitted to Owain that there had been a seriously poor investigation into these two cases. He blamed it on the understaffed police headquarters and the involvement of their senior officer's financial investments with Shedweld.

Superintendent Cadwell had from the start hampered the investigation into Shedweld's business dealings—and now we know why, Owain thought. The missing bullet was the final piece of evidence in the case which proved the inadequate and the lack in proper training of officers concerning the protection of evidence. Incompetence was not the final answer in this case, thought Owain. Even after Cadwell had been removed and disgraced for his involvement in Shedweld's scheme, there was more involvement by this police department's cover-up of evidence and their continued attempt to convict Lady Joanna Whitecoft of the murders. Superintendent Jones continued to pursue her relentlessly. Why? Was he protecting someone, or was he being coerced by Duvrey? Perhaps he was protecting Cadwell and the police detail at headquarters.

Before leaving Sydney, Owain called Jed Hawkins and thanked him for his help with the case. He was on his way to the airport and would be flying out shortly. Because there are no nonstop flights from Australia to the United Kingdom, Owain had a layover in Singapore. At least he was on his way back to Joanna.

Jed Hawkins drove Owain to the airport and they discussed the facts in the case. Jed told Owain that he would follow up the crimes that had been commited by Shedweld and his people along with the obvious involvement of the bank manager. He stopped his police car and helped Wallon on his way. Jed wished him a safe trip home, and hoped that one day he could show Owain what a great place Australia is.

In Singapore, Owain experienced further delays. He had to change planes, and wait for hours before finally boarding his flight to London. While waiting, he had called McDowell on his cell. Fortunately, night or day, McDowell had his cell phoned turned on.

"Sorry to call you like this. I have no idea at the moment what time it is in London."

"Don't worry about it, sir. I know how concerned you are about Lady Joanna. Lord Peter Whitecoft's chauffeur went over to North Wales to bring Mr. Townsend and Lady Joanna back to Lord Peter's townhouse in London. I followed them in my car to make sure that they returned safely. I also called Lord Whitecoft and made him aware of how important you had been in sending me out to investigate the witnesses and the missing bullet. I explained that you were looking into this bank in Perth. He was most grateful for my call. I will meet you at the airport when your plane from Singapore lands."

"How can I thank you for your outstanding police work in this case? I will certainly recommend you for promotion. It seems that I spend more time in planes than anywhere else," said Owain.

Sergeant McDowell was at the waiting area as Chief Inspector Wallon came through customs. He drove Owain over to the Whitecoft townhouse. Lady Joanne had arrived home last night. Her father had explained about Owain coming from Singapore, and that he had invited him to come over to see them. While talking to him, McDowell brought Lord Whitecoft up to date on Shedweld's Family Bank of Perth. He went into what they had found upon arriving at the bank, and then flying out to track down the location of the yacht. Lord Whitecoft had been released from owing any money; his estate was no longer in foreclosure, and the case was now in the hands of Australian agents, who would trace the funds that had been stolen.

Joanna seemed a frail, undernourished woman as she stood before Owain. Her tired eyes with dark circles under them brightened when she saw him.

"I thought my knight had deserted me."

"Never, you know I would never do that. And if you ask I will resign immediately from Scotland Yard and never leave your side again."

They stood holding each other until Lord Peter Whitecroft cleared his throat.

"Oh sir, I'm sorry," Owain said as he turned and shook her father's hand.

"Joanna, if you can bear to let Owain go for just a short while, I believe he looks dead tired and would like to go back to his flat. I asked him over because I have spoken with Sir Gordon and told him that he had to spare Owain to come down to our place in the country where you both can relax. Sir Gordon agreed. So in the morning, why don't you come over here? You and Joanna can drive down together. I believe you have your own car here in London, Owain? I will be up later. Tom and Gwyneth are coming over. We dress for dinner. Bring hiking and casual clothes for daytime. Please don't change the staff's schedule, Joanna. I have everyone instructed as to their duties during our stay." Lord Whitecoft looked tired also but relieved.

Joanna and Owain headed for the door to say goodbye. Kissing and holding on to each other in a long embrace, they knew that this was forever. Owain bent over and whispered in her ear.

"Marry me, my love."

"Yes, oh yes, my love forever," she softly whispered back.

Story of the Welsh Gold Rings

The bright shiny new Bentley had been delivered while Owain was away, as a replacement for the one he had been driving when the rocks rolled down the hillside near Pendol in Wales. Aunt Catherine had seen to the replacement, which was a replica of Owain's old Bentley. Joanna stepped into the car and gazed around in wonder. She had not seen the first one, so this was a surprise for her. Owain skillfully steered the beautiful car down the road and out of London. They sat next to one and another in the front seats talked about their plans as they drove plans. At last, Joanna divulged to Owain her wedding plans.

"Isn't it correct for me to speak to your father first?"

"I already spoke to him, but I guess it would be best if we follow tradition."

"Joanna, he may want to know just how I plan to support you and our family. I have no large inheritance."

"Yes of course, but I have a trust fund, you know. And that should be sufficient if we need more money. I am not planning on an expensive lifestyle. We can be very comfortable; I am sure, with your salary from Scotland Yard."

"Does that include bright red designer dresses, and eating out at expensive French restaurants?" Owain inquired.

"Oh! Please, as long as you keep me in a pair of hiking boots, I will be fine."

Owain could hardly drive, he was laughing so hard. Joanna was giving him directions about where to turn. When they came near the Whitecoft's country estate, she asked Owain to stop the car and pull off to the side of the road. They got out and walked over to view see the distant view of the Georgian-style brick mansion distantly through the trees. The rear view of the large mansion was surrounded with flower beds in bloom. Owain understood why Joanne talked about her fond memories of her childhood home; and he knew he liked what he saw as well.

After driving on, they entered the gates and drove up to the front doors. An elderly butler was there to greet them; and a boy ran up to take care of their luggage. Owain checked to see if he should leave the Bentley where it was, or park it off to the side. The butler explained that the chauffeur would take care of his car.

Upon entering, Owain saw a great staircase ascending on the right side of the hall. The walls were lined with portraits of the family and there were more on the walls of the balcony above. Joanna led him over to the drawing room. A beautiful silver tea service was prepared and set out for them. French doors were open onto a large garden terrace with tables and chairs. Joanna had the butler bring the tea set outside for their enjoyment. The air was warm but some clouds had covered the sun. After relaxing for a short time with their tea, Joanna couldn't help asking, "Well, what do you think? Do you like it?"

"Your home is lovely."

"I hoped that you would like it. Gorwyn Hall has handsome and grand old stone-style architecture. But I worried that you might not like such an English-appearing place as Whitecoft. I spend so much of my time here, and I hope I always will. Wait until you see the stables. My favorite mare is there."

"I'm afraid I don't understand. Your oldest brother will inherit this estate, and you also have another brother who would be in line to inherit the manor as well. *Right?*"

"Oh, yes, you are correct—but Father is very healthy, and my brothers don't show the slightest inclination to marry and settle down at this time. They very much enjoy living in London, and rarely come out here."

"Do I understand you? You want us to live here?"

"No, not exactly, but I really am not very fond of the high society in London. I'm more of a lover of nature, a country girl at heart. Your Aunt Catherine and Uncle Hywel are wonderful people. I love their lifestyle. But I can't imagine that they would want us to move in with them."

"Are you saying that you want us to live here, and I should commute during the week to London? Have you said anything to your father about this plan?" Owain inquired.

"No, I haven't. . . . In fact, I thought it best to go over the idea with you first." Joanna leaned back in her chair and gazed across the lawn to the grand old oak trees. She was wary about looking over at Owain. She might find an expression on his face showing disagreement.

Owain, up to this time, had not given their living location very much thought. He figured that they would find their own place, if not in London, maybe in one of the nice suburbs. This would be a great change of lifestyle for someone such as Joanna, he realized now. She was not the neighbor-across-the-back-fence or meet-at-the-butcher-shop sort of person. Gwyneth, Tom's wife, had loved the idea of living in a cottage behind The Ormes Victoria Hotel. She put her talents for interior decorating and gourmet menu planning to work, and was very successful at it. What about Joanna's interests? She was very intelligent and extroverted with a mind of her own. Obviously, she would need someplace to devote her talents and abilities.

The butler came out to tell them that their rooms were ready. Lord Whitecoft would arrive for lunch around one o'clock. Joanna suggested that they change and go for a walk in the woods and down to the stables.

"Change your shoes. It may be muddy and damp out there. I am sure we will have enough time before Father arrives."

The woods were a pleasant place, and they both forgot about making lifestyle plans. They just walked hand in hand, listening to the birds and taking in the great fresh air. There had not been enough time to see the stables.

After lunch, Lord Whitecoft invited Owain into his library to enjoy a glass of sherry, and of course to have a little talk. Owain started off by asking for Joanna's hand in marriage. He explained how very much in love with Joanna he was. Lord Whitecoft sat quietly listening, and when the appropriate pause in the conversation came, he welcomed Owain to their family and told him that he had admired Owain for some time. He hoped that Joanna and Owain could develop a closer relationship together than he and Joanna's mother had. After the children were born, they more or less went their own ways, except for ceremonial occasions.

It was then that Owain expressed his concern about a place to live that, which would suit Joanna and make her happy. He understood the hereditary aspect and English tradition; this estate which she so dearly loved would not be available to her with two older brothers in line to succeed her.

"She has already spoken to you about this?" inquired Lord Whitecoft.

Owain nodded in the affirmative.

"You are always welcome here while I am alive. But, one of her brothers will inherit the estate. I was afraid that she had that in the back of her mind because her brothers come out here infrequently. You see, there was no problem with her mother, who enjoyed the London social scene. She disliked this place. Joanna grew to love it. I will talk with her. I am sure that some arrangement can be made.

"Ah! I know what is bothering you right now. If you should come to live here, while I am still alive, it would be a long trip for you into Scotland Yard. Again I will make her understand that my estate is a place for you both to come and visit as often as you like. You are especially capable in the handling of people, Owain. I admire you for that. But Joanna will be a challenge for you. However, I have observed you two young people and I feel that you will have a wonderful marriage together."

Out in front of the mansion, a car drove up; Owain could hear Tom's voice as Joanna went out to greet them. Lord Whitecoft rose and motioned for Owain to come along with him and greet the newly arrived guests, Gwyneth and Tom. Everyone entered the hall with laughter and welcoming embraces all around.

Tom approached Owain with a big smile on his face.

"Well, buddy, are congratulations in order?"

Joanna piped up, "Yes." Gwyneth gave her a big hug. Lord Whitecoft had the butler set up the champagne cart. As they entered the beautiful drawing room, Gwyneth looked around in admiration. Lord Peter offered everyone a glass of champagne and toasted the engaged couple.

"We are so happy for you both," Tom said. "Aunt Catherine and Uncle Hywel send their congratulations. They have invited you all to Gorwyn Hall to celebrate. Just give them a little notice." Tom said.

Gwyneth spoke up. "We have news from Michigan. Guy, my brother, and Francesca Montgomery are engaged to be married. Francesca wants to have the wedding in England."

Joanna was so pleased—she had become friends with Francesca, and now they could make wedding plans together. What fun that would be. The men smiled and watched as Gwyneth and Joanna retired to the other end of the room to talk over wedding arrangements.

Tom asked Owain about the outcome of his Australian case. Owain wanted to know about the hotel fire. Lord Whitecoft was also interested in the recovery of Shedweld's investments. His whole financial stability had been threatened by this man, Shedweld. Who killed the man? *The missing bullet, what a mess.*

They were in the midst of this discussion when two young men arrived. Lord Whitecoft went over to greet his sons, Albert, the eldest, and George. Albert greeted his father first while George went over to give his sister a big hug. Lord Whitecoft made the introductions all around; and then he announced the engagement of Owain and Joanna. Both brothers approached Owain to shake his hand and give their sister a kiss. This was the first that they had heard about their sister's beau, as well as the seriousness of the romance. Of course, in their social circle much gossip was making the rounds.

The butler entered and announced that dinner would be at eight and that cocktails would be served in the library beforehand. Everyone left for their rooms. Tom and Owain stayed behind.

"Owain, I have two gifts for you from your aunt and uncle. I think that they would want me to give them to you as soon as possible," Tom said.

Owain looked mystified and wondered what the rush was about. Tom drew two small boxes from his pocket. Also, he handed two envelopes to Owain, and asked him to read the letters inside the envelopes before opening the little packages.

They moved over to a sofa to sit down. Owain opened the envelopes. One was addressed to Owain from his uncle Hywel. The other one was from Aunt Catherine. Tom spoke up, and suggested that maybe he shwould leave. Owain looked up and agreed.

The first letter from Uncle Hywel started out with: "Before you read my letter, please read my sister's letter." Owain put Uncle Hywel's letter on the table with the little packages. He then opened Aunt Catherine's letter:

"When you read this letter, you will understand that we send this gift and our congratulations to you and Joanna. I wanted you to have this gift before you might make a decision about an engagement ring. We love you from the bottom of our hearts, but we denied you your heritage, Owain. This ring was your mother's engagement ring. She loved it so much. The ring belonged to Edward Wallon, your father. Mary Wallon, your father's stepmother, gave this ring to him just before she died. Mary Wallon had received the ring from Edward's mother when Edward was a baby, just before she gave him into the care of Mary Wallon."

Aunt Catherine continued to write that it was her hope that Owain would want to give the ring to Joanna. He opened the little box. Inside was a beautiful gold engraved band with a small emerald set in the top. After carefully studying the ring and the inscription on the inside, Owain set the box down on the table, and picked up the letter from Uncle Hywel:

"This is my greatest joy to give to you *the Welsh gold Templar Knight's signet ring. There is no one more deserving of this ring then you are. Wear it with pride.* Aunt Catherine forgot to mention that *the little engagement ring that our sister Elizabeth received from your father was also made from Welsh gold;* only close members of the royal family were allowed to have rings of Welsh gold. This was an heirloom ring from your grandmother's family."

Owain took the two rings up to his room and laid them on the table next to his bed. He then went to take a bath before dinner. As he relaxed in the bath, he wondered how close Joanna's room was to his.

After dressing for dinner in his new dinner jacket, he carefully took the gold signet ring out of its box and put the ring on the little finger of his right hand and gazed upon the ring with a strong feeling of pride. How long had it been put away and not worn? His mother's engagement ring he put in the pocket of his jacket.

Just then a knock came on his bedroom door, and he knew it had to be Joanna. She entered dressed in a lovely light blue soft flowing full length gown. Around her neck she wore a single strand of beautiful pearls, with pearl earrings to match. Her hair was curled in little ringlets around her face with a light blue ribbon on top. The blue matched the sparkling blue of her eyes. She took his arm as they headed down the stairs to join everyone in the drawing room. They glided in to meet the guests almost as if they were walking on air, and everyone stood up to greet the lovely couple.

Albert walked over to admire the strand of pearls that Joanna was wearing around her neck. "Those are Mother's, aren't they?" he asked stiffly.

"No," Lord Whitecoft quickly spoke, as he approached Joanna, "they are *my* mother's pearls. This is the perfect occasion to give them to my daughter."

Realizing the moment was becoming strained between father and son, Owain stepped closer to Joanna. "This . . . is the occasion to give you a ring to celebrate our engagement." From his pocket he removed the little gold ring with the emerald on top, and reached for Joanna's left hand.

"May this ring be a symbol of my love for you, Joanna. *The emerald is the green of the forest, and the gold is from the earth of Wales. My aunt Catherine wanted me to have this ring, to give to you tonight.* My mother received this ring from my father, and he received it as an heirloom from his mother. Mary Wallon, his stepmother, kept the ring for him until he was to marry. Aunt Catherine kept the ring for me until I was to marry."

Albert looked over at his father and George. "May I have a look at the special ring from Owain's family?"

"Of course, you can," Joanna answered her brother.

Joanna started to take off the ring to hand it to her brother.

"Don't take it off. It looks so beautiful on your finger," Lord Whitecoft said.

Albert reached for his sister's hand to take a closer look at the little ring and said, "I thought only the royal family could have rings made from Welsh gold?"

"That's true, but my gold signet ring from the fourteenth century was made from Welsh gold," said Owain as he raised his right hand for others to see . . . "and was presented to a Templar Knight of Wales named Owain Pentwyn y Gruffydd. This ring is one of a pair which was a gift to the twin brothers who excelled in their duty to the church. The other ring is in Gwyneth's family."

Albert turned while holding Joanna's hand, and for the first time took a good look at Owain. Recognition appeared on Albert's face as he realized who it was that Owain so keenly resembled.

Then, Lord Peter Whitecoft broke in to say, "I went to Oxford with William Pentwyn Lydley, Gwyneth's father, who has the other Welsh gold signet ring, and we are good friends. ," mentioned Lord Whitecoft. "Francesca Montgomery is engaged to Guy Pentwyn Lydley. They will be coming to England soon. Francesca is the sister of Sir Harold Montgomery, who I'm sure you have met before."

"George, your mouth is open," said his brother, Albert.

Both brothers were hearing this news for the first time. Their social lives had them traveling in circles of the titled nobility. George, who had not had the opportunity of looking at the two rings, approached Joanna and Owain.

"*Well, well, Father, you have been keeping much from us,*" -Albert commented as George nodded in agreement.

"No.... No. It was not my intention to do so," Lord Peter Whitecoft replied.

The butler entered and announced dinner.

Joanna moved up to her father and took his arm. "Father, please let us have peace and understanding in this family. I realize that your sons have not always shown enough concern for your feelings. They may feel left out. Mother had a very strong influence on them. She might have disapproved of Owain. However, this is the best time to clear the air, please." Joanna whispered this softly to her father as they left the drawing room and entered the beautiful candlelit dining room.

"Yes, yes, you are so right; and we will repair our family rela-
tionships, I promise you. I should have spoken to your brothers
about your probable engagement before this." Lord Peter smiled
down at Joanna.

Albert and George did not stay the night. They both begged off
due to previous set engagements. Tom and Gwyneth left first thing
in the morning after breakfast. They too, had responsibilities to
attend to at the hotel. Before leaving, they encouraged Owain and
Joanna to come down and spend weekends at the shore; Catherine
and Hywel would be excited to see them also.

Joanna was anxious to show Owain the stables and her favorite
mare, Dancing Lady. Horses were not an interest of Owain's. His
sports interests had centered on rugby and mountain climbing;
horseback riding skills were not one of them. Joanna was not going
to let that get in the way. She looked forward to teaching Owain
horsemanship. Owain had shown very little interest in becoming
proficient in equestrian accomplishments. Horseback riding was
considered a gentleman's activity.

Joanna brought out one of her brother's sets of riding clothes
that she felt would fit him. Owain looked at the apparel with misgivings. Love conquers all, however, and after changing into the outfit,
Joanna and Judd, the stable manager, coached Owain into mounting a very calm old mare which Judd had saddled and brought into
the ring.

Owain became even more doubtful that this was an appropriate activity for him. Joanna encouraged her student. She
knew that he was a very coordinated and talented sportsman and
she had confidence that he would take to horseback riding easily; they could soon go out on the trails of her father's estate
together.

After Owain watched Joanna mount her mare, Owain mount-
ed. Judd cautiously led the old mare around the ring. With years
of experience, Judd spoke the instructions to Owain in a way that
would not be overbearing or insulting to him. Owain responded,
and was quick to learn. By the time the old mare had made several turns around the ring, his confidence level had risen. Maybe
this would not be a bad idea, after all. He knew that his uncle Hywel's eyebrows would rise at the thought of his nephew taking up

horseback riding. In his eyes, one used dogs to control sheep, not horses. There were no stables at Gorwyn Hall.

Joanna and Owain spent the better part of the afternoon on horseback. Judd liked this fellow, and felt that he had the talent to become a very talented horseman. He took to the saddle, and controlling and guiding the horse came naturally. The old mare responded immediately to his commands.

Joanna suggested, "Owain, I think you are doing really well. Shall we go in for afternoon tea? My father is probably wondering where we are. I know he plans to leave first thing in the morning for London. Dismount, and bring your clothes with you up to the house. You can change again in your room."

Owain took one step forward after dismounting, and realized that horseback riding worked muscles that he had not been using recently. It took all of his masculine pride to keep from limping. "Right, tea would be just the thing, and I am famished," Owain announced.

Sitting on the veranda, observing Owain and Joanna approach, Lord Peter Whitecoft watched with amusement as Owain did his very best to ignore the discomfort that he must feel after being four hours on a horse for the first time. He ordered the butler to bring more sandwiches with some cheese and roast beef.

"Well, well, you two. Come and join me. Oh, don't bother, Owain, you can change after you have had some nice sandwiches and tea. Riding attire is quite fine for tea on the veranda," said Lord Peter.

Owain gently lowered his aching body into one of the soft cushioned chairs. Joanna plopped down next to him and proceeded to tell her father about Owain's new found talent as a horseman. Her father smiled at both of them, and offered Owain refreshments. Owain wondered to himself, if it would be possible for him to stand and walk again. After glasses of sherry, tea, and six sandwiches, he excused himself and made for his room and a nice hot bath. The butler took care of everything. The maids had his bath ready and took away his riding clothes. He had plenty of towels and a nice fresh robe and slippers for his use.

After dinner, sitting in the drawing room, Lord Peter said, "Joanna, the staff have their instructions and you are, please, not to go around confusing them. They are very competent to handle everything. Just let them know your schedule, and let them do their duties. I am sure that this can be a very relaxing and enjoyable time for you both. Now, Judd will have stables ready for your use, and you have Owain's Bentley to travel around and see some of the beautiful country in this part of England, if you wish. Please let Benton know your plans for meals. I am retiring now since I want to get away early."

Lord Peter rose and said good night. "Don't worry about seeing me off in the morning."

Who Killed Shedweld?

The next morning, Joanna awoke and realized that it was late. She hopped out of bed and dressed quickly. Then she planned to run down to Owain's room to see if he had overslept too or was already awake and dressed for breakfast. Out in the hall, she could have sworn that she heard her brother Albert calling to the servants and asking about his missing riding attire. She knew that Benton, the butler, had had little time to clean the riding outfit that she had given Owain to wear yesterday. Joanna quickly returned to her room to put on her clothes. She knew Albert would be furious with her for lending his riding clothes to someone else. She proceeded down the stairs to greet her brother. Owain was nowhere in sight. He was probably still in his room.

"Hello, Albert, I was not expecting you. Father left this morning, but said nothing about you coming back."

"That's because I didn't tell him," Albert answered his sister's anxious enquiry. "I plan to bring a few of the fellows from my club here for the week."

"Didn't Father tell you that Owain and I were staying here for the week?"

"No! . . . Not that I can remember. Well, you had better pack up your things and head back into London. This bunch of friends I have invited are not your type, old girl."

"That's not fair; Father gave me permission to stay here, first. You can't just throw us out because you are bringing down some of your rowdy friends from London."

"Well, stay then—you do know that my fellows like to smoke, drink a lot, and stay up to all hours. You and your new fellow—what is his name? Oh! Yes, Owain, the Welshman . . . is welcome to a join the party." Joanna was furious. She knew that Owain would not like Albert's friends.

Just then, coming out of the library was none other than Louis Duvrey. Joanna glared at him and demanded to know what he was doing here. Duvrey grinned at her, and was about to go over to give her a kiss on her cheek when Owain appeared at the top of the balcony and headed down the steps towards them.

Louis Duvrey stepped back showing some surprise at seeing Owain there. Albert immediately stepped forward and asked if Owain and Duvrey knew each other. Duvrey turned towards the library; but Owain made it to the library door first.

"Louis Duvrey, you are wanted for questioning at Scotland Yard Headquarters concerning your involvement with Dirk Otis Shedwell's illegal financial ventures," he said firmly.

"Are you going to arrest me, Chief Inspector Wallon?" Duvrey smirked as he glared at Owain.

"No, I am officially informing you that Chief Superintendent Sir William Gordon wants you to come in for questioning. You can come on your own, or—"

At that moment, Albert, his face beet red, reached the library door, and demanded Owain leave his house immediately and announced that Owain was out of line to speak to his friend, Louis Duvrey in that manner. "You are not allowed to conduct your police work in my house," Albert informed Owain.

"I am sorry, Albert, this is an important police matter, and your friend is wanted at headquarters for questioning involving a serious criminal investigation."

Standing in the hallway was the butler and half of the servant staff. "Forcibly throw this man out!" shouted Albert to Benton the butler.

Joanna ran over to stand between her brother and Owain. She was afraid that there was going to be a fight. Her brother was a blathering idiot if he didn't know what this man Louis had tried to do to her and their father.

"Please, Joanna, wait for me in my car, we are leaving immediately," said Owain as he stepped towards the front door. Outside he turned on his cell phone and reported to the authorities that Louis Duvrey was at the Whitecoft Hall and was wanted by Scotland Yard for questioning about his involvement in crimes committed in Australia.

Joanna ran to the garage where the Bentley was parked. Owain followed her, still talking on his cell to the authorities as he reached his car. Keys in hand, he started the engine and drove the car out through the main gates of the Whitecoft estate.

"Joanna, is there a back entrance to your father's estate?"

"Why, yes, there is." Joanna answered.

Sir Gordon was calling Owain on his cell to warn him of the danger that he and Joanna were in. Sir Gordon's instructions were for Owain to leave the area and return to headquarters. Duvrey had a license for a gun. Gordon knew that Owain was unarmed, and had Joanna with him. Owain understood the danger. He headed the Bentley back to London. The local police passed them as they were on their way to apprehend Duvrey.

Upon arriving at Scotland Yard Headquarters, Owain and Joanna were escorted into a meeting room near Sir Gordon's office. Waiting for them, in the meeting room was Joanna's father, Lord Whitecoft. He had been apprised of the serious events occurring at his estate. He knew about the involvement of Duvrey in Shedweld's illegal business matters, which included the foreclosure attempt on his estate. He did not know that his son, Albert was a friend of Duvrey's. That shocked and hurt him deeply. He could not understand how his son did not know about his financial difficulties, and poor Joanna's arrest. Of course, his son, Albert had been hunting in Africa until just the other day and probably did not realize what had been happening.

Sir Gordon explained to them, "Duvrey got away. He had his plane standing by at a local small private airport. The police chased him to the air strip, but before they could stop him, he had boarded his plane and taken off. We are tracking the plane now. The Australian police have a warrant out for his arrest. They have enough evidence to convict him on several criminal charges. One is attempted murder."

Lord Whitecoft spoke up. "Where is Albert? Did he go with Duvrey?"

"No," said Sir Gordon. "He is not wanted by us, and there are no charges against him. I'm so sorry, Lord Peter, that this occurred on your property after all that you have been through, dear friend."

Joanna went over to her father and said, "I want to stay with you in town for now, please."

Sir Gordon explained to them that he needed Owain, his chief inspector, to return to North Wales with Sgt. McDowell and to finish the investigation. He had received information concerning Shedwelds real murderer.

After the meeting, Owain drove Joanna and her father back to Lord Whitecoft's townhouse. He was invited for lunch. They were all in somewhat of a daze. Lord Peter announced that he would speak with Albert; and Joanna was not to talk with Albert for a while. Lord Peter knew that Albert socialized with a wild group from his club, and that they were into gambling and rowdy parties. Albert and he had not been on very good terms for a while and obviously Albert was not aware of Duvrey's involvement in the financial scandal.

Lord Peter planned to call his butler at his country estate to make sure everything had settled down. His chauffeur would bring Owain's suitcase over to his flat in London. Lord Peter took his daughter's hand with the engagement ring on it and gently kissed it. Joanna put her arms around her father to comfort him. Owain rose to leave and Joanna accompanied him to the door.

"I must say good-bye for now, but I'll call you tonight. The plan is that I'll go to The Ormes Victoria Hotel to stay tonight. It would be best if you stayed here, but if you decide to go back to the Whitecoft estate, let me know."

After kissing Owain goodbye, Joanna closed the office door and leaned against it and cried.

Owain left his Bentley in town and took a police car, with Sgt. McDowell at the wheel. They drove to North Wales police headquarters. McDowell told his boss that a new man had been put in charge. Inspector Jones was back at his old job. Morale at the station was pretty low. Cadwell's whereabouts were not known. Jones wanted Wallon and McDowell to accompany him up to a small farm on the west coast of Scotland to talk with Cadwell's wife. She'd requested that they come see her, Jones told him.

Mrs. Cadwell was waiting for Jones, McDowell, and Chief Inspector Wallon at the farm door when the three men arrived. She invited them in for a cup of tea and biscuits. As they sat at the table, Mrs. Cadwell told them. Her husband confessed to what happened at Shedweld's cottage the morning of his murder.

"Edwin had gone up to help Shedweld empty out his cottage. He had already delivered the treasure from the security room to the cottage, as Shedweld had ordered him to do. My husband wanted the money back that he had invested in Shedweld's scheme. Edwin was told that he could not have his money back, and to keep his mouth shut." Mrs. Cadwell rubbed tears from her eyes. She continued with Edwin's confession.

"My husband was furious. He knew he would lose his job if Shedweld turned him in, which Shedweld had threatened to do before. At that moment, they heard a car coming up the driveway. Shedweld went out to see who it was. A young blond-haired man was yelling at Shedweld something about destroying Mother Earth, Edwin told me. Shedweld laughed at the young blond haired man and turned away. Then, the young man pulled out a pistol and shot at him. My husband, Edwin, told me that he missed. Shedweld panicked and dropped to the ground. Edwin watched the young man run to his car and drive away. Then my husband told me that he pulled his pistol out of his pocket as Shedweld stood up and shot him in the back. He didn't miss. Shedweld lay dead next to his car in the driveway."

"Edwin explained to me that he would not be blamed for killing Shedweld because the blond young man thought *he* had killed Shedweld and would be arrested for murder. Later, Edwin called me on the telephone and told me to leave him, that he was no good. I was to go up to my sister's farm. I packed my things and left for my sister's immediately. I had no idea then if I would ever see him again. When Edwin arrived at my door, he looked terrible. That's when he confessed. The next morning"—

"Where is your husband now?" McDowell asked Mrs. Cadwell.

"He's dead. They found his boat out at sea, and his body float-ing nearby. We buried him up on the hill. You can go up there and see the grave. He was a good husband to me."

"What day did you see him before he went out in the boat? Asked Jones, he was completely shocked by this story.

Mrs. Cadwell was stammering, "Yes, you are right. My husband wanted to see me. The police put him under house arrest for drink-ing on duty and leaving his police responsibilities. His own men turned him in." She said with bitterness.

"I don't remember the date when he arrived. I was so scared when I found out; and he didn't want me involved, and not to tell anyone about it. Up here in this little fishing village, people don't know much about other places. They knew that Edwin was in trou-ble but they just minded their own business, like they always did," said Mrs. Cadwell.

Wallon spoke up and turned to Jones for some answers. "When did you find out this information?"

"Mrs. Cadwell called the station. She told me that her husband was dead; and she had something important to say about Shed-weld's murder. I did not know what to expect. Then I contacted Sir Gordon at Scotland Yard yesterday. He told me that you would be coming to Wales right away." Jones told them.

"You said that your husband went out in a boat. Did you know where he was going, and if he had a gun with him?" McDowell questioned Mrs. Cadwell. He was concerned about the pistol that killed Shedwell.

"He just went out with the idea of killing himself. I didn't ask any questions or look for any gun," she was almost histerical by this time as the tears poured down her cheeks.

"What about his pistol? Did he have his police pistol when he arrived at you farm?" asked McDowell.

"Oh, I don't know…. He was a good man. I don't know how that evil man Shedweld tricked Edwin into giving him all our savings."

"Thank you, Mrs. Cadwell, for calling us. You did the right thing. We will turn in your signed statement," said Chief Inspector Wallon. "The courts will want you to give them an official state-ment. His grave will be investigated along with others who were at the burial. You understand that we will have to search your house. We can do it now or comeback later with a court order."

She invited them to search the farm house and she brought out all of Edwin's belongings that she had. After they searched the house the pistol was found in the pocket of his uniform. They left Scotland with her signed statement and headed for Wales. The Police in Scotland would be told and she would have to make a statement to them as well.

Inspector Jones said very little on the return trip. He told Wallon he did not know where Edwin had gone and was so busy with the murder case that he did not do the right thing. Edwin Cadwell was his best friend. He should never have pursued the investigation of Lady Joanna. Unfortunately Mr. Duvrey had been so positive that she was guilty. Mr. Duvrey and his lawyers were very convincing.

Owain Wallon sat quietly in the back of the car. Then he gave the order for McDowell to go directly to Shedweld's cottage. He told them that he wanted to look for the bullet that didn't hit Shedweld. It should still be up there in the area near the cottage. With that bullet there would be no doubt that Glyn Anderson did not kill Shedweld. It was getting dark; but Owain was determined to make a stab at finding the bullet right away. McDowell parked the car, and they went over to where Shedweld's car had been parked at the time of the murder.

"The bullet did not hit the car, or else we would have found it. Jones,– you be Shedweld and stand next to where the car was. If Professor Anderson was over here, away from his car . . . McDowell, you go up there where we think Cadwell could have been standing. Shedweld had his back to both of them. Cadwell's bullet went into Shedweld's back after Anderson fired and missed. Jones, make sure your back is to McDowell and I will try to figure out where Anderson's bullet could have gone after he missed Shedweld's back," said Owain as he stepped to where Anderson may have been standing when he shot at Shedweld and missed. Remember, Anderson was not experienced with firearms but Cadwell was."

The three of them looked in the direction of the path that Anderson's bullet would have taken. *A wooden fence was there.* Taking out their torches they made their way over to the fence. Jones spotted the bullet imbedded in the fence. Carefully, McDowell dug the bullet out of the wooden fence. They returned to the police car and drove back to headquarters.

"I am sending the bullet to our London labs for a ballistics test. Jones, you do have Anderson's pistol?" Owain looked over at Jones with a firm tone to his voice *"Now, we have Cadwell's pistol to send along* with this bullet."

"Yes, of course, I will get his pistol for you to send along as well," said Jones, and he left to bring up Anderson's pistol from their evidence room. Jones looked very demoralized.

The new superintendent of the district headquarters was listening, as well as most of the officers. They realized that there could be no doubt that Cadwell; their previous boss had committed the crime. Jones confessed that Cadwell held a grudge against Lady Joanna Whitecoft when she made a fool out of Jones back at the cave entrance when she took the key and the locked the cave door. Owain was disturbed to think that a grudge could go so far as to try and convict her of murder.

Two days later, they had the lab's analysis. The two bullets were from Anderson's pistol. He had fired the first bullet that they found in the fence. The second bullet had been fired when he took his own life. The bullet that killed Shedweld was from Cadwell's pistol, which was the same caliber as Anderson's. Both guns were correctly registered to their owners. The authorities discussed exhuming Shedweld's body to locate Cadweld's bullet. An exhumation order was sent to Sydney, Australia. They were waiting for an answer.

The police officers at headquarters had a difficult time accepting the murder and then suicide of their boss, Edwin Cadwell. They took up a collection for his widow. The case against Lady Joanna Whitecoft was permanently closed. The friends of Glyn Anderson were thankful that he had not actually killed Shedweld. However, he did kill for Mother Earth when he killed Sutter. *It was a sad case.*

Louis Duvrey slipped away again. Australia had standing warrants for his arrest. Sir Gordon was convinced that Duvrey and Shedweld's gang had escaped with the funds from the Perth bank and maybe other funds as well. The investors were after Duvrey. He was believed to be in the Far East, joined up with another operation of Asian crooks. The British police were watching for him should he try and slip into England again.

Sir Albert Whitecoft had been thoroughly informed about the dangers of being entangled with or giving support in any way to Louis Duvrey. His father, Lord Whitecoft, had threatened to disown him if he went to Duvrey's aid again. Albert apologized to his sister, Joanna and her fiancé for the way he had acted that day at the Whitecoft estate. He was very supportive of Owain's interest in horseback riding. He told them. "I have been out of touch in Africa and didn't pay a bit of attention when I returned to the stories going around."

The double wedding plans were going forward. Francesca and Joanna, along with Gwyneth, planned a spectacular affair. First to be settled were all the choices for the parties preceding the wedding day. The invitation lists had been compiled. The Whitecoft estate had spacious formal rooms for a very large wedding reception, which appeared to be the best plan. Tom and Gwyneth encouraged the wedding couples to have parties at their hotel. Both the Montgomerys and the Whitecofts preferred England to Wales, but then that was to be expected. Owain intervened on behalf of Aunt Catherine and settled the matter. Owain wanted his bachelor party for his old chums to be at The Ormsby Victoria Hotel. Guy Lydley thought that was a great idea; and since his family and friends were coming over from America and would be staying at the same hotel, it would work out well.

The Lydley parents and their friends had been invited to Gorwyn Hall, where more parties were to be held. Catherine accepted the plans graciously. This left the Montgomery brothers to entertain their out-of-town guest in London. This would leave the Whitecoft's lovely place free for the girls and their part of the wedding party for a place to have fun and rest before the big day.

The plans worked splendidly and to everyone's satisfaction. The brides and bridesmaids looked wonderful, even though they had been partying most of the night. The ceremony in the little chapel on the Whitecoft estate was packed; but most everyone found a place to sit. Bride and groom traveled from the chapel in a large flower-bedecked carriage of four horses and attendants appropriately dressed in livery attire. The guests paraded behind. Those who were not up to the walking were provided with carriages as well. As the guests reached Whitecoft Hall, trumpets sounded; and they all entered to enjoy a great reception.

Afterwards the Lydleys, Guy and Francesca left for their honeymoon in New Orleans. The Wallons, Owain and Joanna were to spend their honeymoon on a private island in the Bahamas. Lord Whitecoft had a school buddy who had made a fortune in the Far East and owned one of the small islands near Bimini. Both couples planned to meet in New Orleans at the end of their honeymoons for a couple of days and then return home. Guy and Francesca planned to live near his parents in Michigan. Owain and Joanna had leased a small flat in London. Owain would be staying in his position as chief inspector for Scotland Yard's Special Branch.

Old Cave Revisited

Following their honeymoon in the Bahamas, Owain and Joanna returned to their flat in London. Soon, however, Joanna became very impatient and frustrated with her day-to-day life. Her friends were out gallivanting about in their usual daily pursuit of social activities, clubs, and shopping. This was not an environment which Joanna wanted to join. She missed Snowdonia and her activities there. Owain's time was completely filled with new investigations into the illegal drug business. Finally, one weekend they decided that both of them needed a change of scenery and took off for The Ormes Victoria Hotel.

The weather was wet and damp. The hotel was full of London partyers trying to escape for the weekend, only to be disappointed when they realized that hiking in damp, muddy outfits over wet trails was not for them. So everyone sat around and partied in the lounge and restaurant all day and all night. The hotel made money, but this atmosphere was exactly what Joanna was hoping to escape. Owain was also disappointed. He wanted to see his friends. But both Tom and Gwyneth were kept busy attending to the guests. Owain wanted to relax and have time to be with Joanna away from the stress of London and the crime cases at the Yard.

Joanna sat with him in the lounge, completely bored. She had hoped that the rain would stop and they could go hiking on one of the trails near the hotel.

"I have an idea," said Joanna. "Let's go check out that damp old cave. Glyn had been investigating the markings on the walls and floor. I heard that Glyn's colleagues Brian and Edward recently found some interesting objects that they can't identify."

"That's crazy," said Owain, who was not interested in going back into the gruesome dark cave where the bodies and skeletons had been found.

"Well you wouldn't want to go into a damp old cave on a sunny day, would you?" asked Joanna. "Bet the chaps from the archeology team are there today. Do you remember them? They have classes to teach at university during the week. Well, I think that is better than sitting around here. Do you think Gwyneth can get away? I know that Tom will not be able to leave." Commented Joanna as she proceeded to the hotel phone.

Joanna had not been in the cave before. To Owain, the thought of returning there after all that they had been through seemed somewhat odd. Owain realized that Joanna was thinking about Glyn again. She had been very fond of Glyn and with his suicide before her very eyes she still was troubled about everything. Glyn confided in her about his interest in the writing and marks on the cave wall. He felt that this cave had been used for many many centuries. Brian and Edward had apparently returned to the cave to carry on Glyn's work.

Owain reached out for Joanna's hand and suggested. "First call the university and find out if Brian and Edward have gone to the site today." Owain added. "We could of course go to Gorwyn Hall to see Aunt Catherine and Uncle Hywel, you know." Owain called after Joanna who was on her way to the telephone.

"But, they would expect us to pack up and go stay with them," Joanna called back to Owain.

"Yes, I suppose you are right." He wanted to please her after all she had been through. Glyn had been an old friend and after what had happened she wanted to encourage Glyn's archeology studies of the cave. Yes, he had gone crazy at the end but up until that time he was known as an outstanding geologist.

Gwyneth came over to join Owain while Joanna made her inquiries.

"You know, Owain, she was fascinated with that cave and the items that Glyn always talked about. From the moment he entered the cave, you told us, he wanted to investigate the markings on the side walls and he felt that the floor of the cave was superficially filled-in earth to cover a previous investigation. And then there were the blackened stains on parts of the walls, leading him to believe that fires had been lit there. The opening from the other side, which Tom and I found that day, while sheltering away from the storm could have served as the draft chimney for the fires.

Owain put down his paper as Joanna, with a gleeful expression on her face, approached them. He knew that he was outnumbered and might as well accept the *idea of cave-trudging on a rainy afternoon.*

"Yes, they are there and planning to work for the rest of the day. I cannot reach them by cell in that cave; but I don't think that we are making a mistake to drive out there. Let's change our clothes and leave," Joanna said with glee.

Gwyneth headed for the kitchen to have a basket of sandwiches, wine, and hot coffee prepared. Tom grumbled when he heard the news. "It's raining and damp out there and you want to go have a picnic in a dreary old cave?" Owain looked over at Tom and smirked.

After loading up the Land Rover, the three of them took off for the inland region where the cave was located. The area was clearly marked "Keep Out", but they continued up the well-traveled dirt road. Upon arriving at the entrance, one of the researchers came out to see who was coming. Recognizing Owain, Brian came over to help take one of the baskets of food and refreshment out of the back of the Land Rover.

"Great to see you, but you must understand that we cannot contaminate the cave." Then after inspecting what was in the basket, Brian quickly added, "Of course with all this wonderful food, there is a place along the far side where we have set up a trailer for such purposes. Follow me."

He led them to a fenced-off area on the far side of the cave opening where a trailer was being used as a makeshift laboratory. Joining them was the team leader Brian, the archeologist of the group. Edward, who was showing them around the large well-equipped trailer, was the anthropologist. Glyn Anderson who committed suicide had been the geologist on the team, which he had organized. Both Brian and Edward were trying to recover from the terrible loss of their friend. They felt that the best thing to do was to continue on with the investigation of the cave.

"Well, what do you think of our off-site laboratory?" asked Brian as Joanna looked over a collection of small pieces of stone that appeared to have designs on them. Brian called out to her, "Now, Joanna, please don't pick up or move those pieces."

"Oh!—I won't, but I have pieces that look just like some of these pieces that you have on the table."

"Really!" exclaimed Brian. He moved closer to find out which pieces Joanna had found that were similar to the pieces on the table. As he approached, she looked up and said, "These items here are similar to others that I found in the Bahamas off the coast of Florida where Owain and I spent our honeymoon."

"You found stones like these on the beach?" Brian asked incredulously.

"No, not on the beach," answered Joanna, "but on a small rise with some kind of a round stone building at the center. The natives told us that the stone structure was supposed to be a lighthouse at one time. We asked about the age of the building but they had no idea. They just told us that it was long before their families arrived on the island. There were lots of these stones around the base of this old building, and I picked a couple of the most interesting ones to bring back with me."

"Good Lord, you mean that there were many pieces?" Brian asked.

"Why, yes, of course that is what I meant," answered Joanna.

Everyone came over to look at the small oblong pieces with tiny scratch-like marks on them. Brian and Edward looked at one another and then at Joanna. "Where are the pieces that you brought back to London?"

"In a small box along with other trinkets that I had collected on the hill and down by the beach while Owain went out fishing. I can bring them back next weekend if you like, and then you can take a look at them."

"No, that won't be necessary; if it is alright with you, I will come to London the first of the week," said Brian.

"Of course it is. We would love to have you come see us."

"No, I won't be staying; but thank you for inviting me. I need to visit some people at the British Museum."

"I'm hungry," said Owain. "Let's open the baskets. Have the two of you had lunch and can you stop at this point?"

"Why yes, we can and afterwards we will take you on a guided tour of our project." They all grabbed stools and chairs and enjoyed the basket of sandwiches, wine, little cakes, and coffee. Because it was getting late and the rain had not let up, they made their way to the cave and the tour that they had been promised.

As the group entered the main room of the cave they could make out the marked-off places that were being carefully examined.

"Over here inside this large excavated hole is where we found the pieces of stone that you found so interesting. Unfortunately the cave is very difficult to date. Many of the places that you see around the base of the walls were debris mounds from different periods of habitation. As each group of tenants moved in to use the cave, they shoveled the leftovers from the previous peoples who had occupied the cave into piles against the walls. We speculate that there have been many articles left here for hundreds if not thousands of years."

"Are you serious?" asked Owain. "You are estimating that peo-ple have been using the cave as far back as the Stone Age."

"Yes, but understand that this is speculation on our part; and we still have much work to do to substantiate the dates. The age of some of the items that can be carbon-dated indicated that it was used at one time just after the last ice age. However, there are long periods between when the cave may not have been used and was completely deserted."

"Amazing," said Joanna. "What a find you have here."

Gwyneth had not stayed with the others but wandered off to another part of the cave where Brian and Edward had not started to excavate. *She was bending down and putting her hands against the wall and then against the floor, her vision was clear to her now. She seemed to be upset while doing it. She rose up and spoke to the others.*

"Maybe it would be best if you did not disturb this place," Gwyneth suggested. "There is much sadness here. I can feel it," she insisted.

Joanna went over and held her friend's hand. "Gwyneth and her brother Guy both have claims to psychic powers. She must be sensing something," said Joanna.

"Come," said Owain, "and bring Gwyneth with you." He encouraged because making assumption based on visions was not what he wanted to start investigating at this time. "We must return to the hotel. Tom will be looking for us." He started for the entrance and the Land Rover. They all thanked Brian and Edward for the tour. Their hosts thanked them for the basket lunch and wine.

"I will see you next week in London, but I will give you a call to make sure that you are available. I am very interested to see those stones and other objects you mentioned, that you have collected from that island in the Caribbean," said Brian.

Driving back to the hotel, Joanna asked Gwyneth if she could explain any more about what she had felt back in the cave. Owain cleared his throat and looked over at Joanna, who took his hint; and changed the subject of their conversation.

Later, after they had had dinner, Joanna and Gwyneth sat together in the hotel lounge.

"I can try and explain what I felt." Gwyneth continued to tell Joanna about her vision. "The image came to me of a young girl who lay dying in the cave. There were many people around her who were also dying. They were dressed in beautiful garments that could not keep them warm and the place was very cold and getting colder all the time. A man sat near her while he made impressions on a stone tablet with some sort of instrument. That was all that I could gather at the time but I think the impressions that he was making on the stone tablet were like those on the small pieces we looked at in the lab. Maybe Brian and Edward had found pieces of that tablet in the cave. A male figure was also slowly dying, of cold, I think."

Joanna said, "All that we can do for now is to wait for Brian to come to London and look at the pieces I found on the island in the Bahamas."

Owain and Joanna returned to London the next day and Joanna waited for a contact from Brian. While waiting she decided to examine the collection of items that she had gathered on their honeymoon. She pulled out recent photos that she and Owain had taken on their honeymoon. She hoped that some of them might show the remains of the stone tower on the hill and also places that she had been to collect the small items that had caught her interest.

Monday, Brian called from the British Museum artifact labs. He wanted to come over right away. She agreed and then went into the small kitchen that they had at their London flat to make tea. Just as she finished preparing her new tea service, the bell rang. Joanna went to the door to greet Brian.

"Hello Brian, you made good time. I have the items you requested to see on the table in our parlor."

Brian rushed in and handed Joanna his umbrella. It was pouring outside. They went into the parlor and Joanna brought in the tea tray and poured Brian a cup.

"Oh, how splendid of you, I could sure use a cup of hot tea. The labs were very interested in my pieces of stone with the markings that I showed you. They cannot identify the stone and it may not be stone at all but composite of another material that looks like stone and is very solid. The technicians at the lab did not think that the markings were made by any kind of tool used centuries ago. They had the idea that the markings were made with a laser tool. No one had laser tools centuries ago."

"So." Putting on his eyeglasses, Brian examined the pieces that were on the table. "I think we have a close match here. Without all the equipment I need to examine these specimens, I can't say for sure." Brian started examining the other items Joanna had arranged on the table. Carefully, he turned each one over and asked Joanna again where they had been found.

"I have some shots that we took of the places where I found the items. Here is the one of the stone tower on the hill. Most of the island was very flat. The other pictures are of the beach near where we stayed."

"What a beautiful spot. I have never been to the Bahamas and would love to go. Look at the color of the water and the white sand." Brian studied the picture of the stone tower, or what was left of it. "This does not resemble recent construction. Do the islanders know about the history of the place?"

"They could not give us very much information except to say it was old. They thought maybe pirates had built it during the time when pirates used the island."

"How do they know it was pirates?"

"Everyone in that area likes to tell stories about pirates and hidden treasure. The visitors to the islands love to hear these stories. However, there is something else that an old man likes to tell and of course that's maybe another tale. He says that aliens come out of the sky to visit this island. You realize that he is speculating about *the tales of the Bermuda Triangle.*"

"Of course," remarked Brian. "Has anyone taken the time to investigate the ruins of the tower and ground around it?"

"Obviously, I did. That is where I found these pieces that I am showing you now. And there were a lot more of them inside and outside the tower."

"Could you go in and did the tower have a cover?"

"Yes, yes it did. Most of the stone covering had fallen down. Evidently, someone must have used the area for a while and built a covering for it. There was a ladder on the outside. It was not very old."

"What do you suppose they used the tower for?"

"Oh, I can't imagine; it may have been used by the island children for playing pirate games."

The door to the flat opened and Owain walked in to join them. "Well, Brian, have you investigated Joanna's collection? The immigration official didn't know quite what to make of these odd trinkets and decided Joanna had not damaged or taken something that could be considered destroying ancient artifacts."

Brian laughed and said, "*These objects that she has collected, especially the ones that resemble the items that I found in the cave back in Wales appear to be connected to some form of ancient communication.* I say communication rather than writing because I have never observed anything like them before. The technicians at the museum labs were stumped also. They ventured the notion that the marks were made by some type of laser tool on an object which was not stone."

"Laser markings, not stone? What does this mean?" Owain asked.

"I'm not sure; however, I plan on returning tomorrow to the cave to search for more of these items. Can I take your pieces with me?"

"Why, yes, of course you may," said Joanna. "I will be anxious know what comes of all this. Oh, by the way, Gwyneth told me the story of her vision while in the cave. What is especially interesting was that she had the feeling that a man, at least she thought that he was a man, had been marking these tablets with some kind of tool. He moved the piece that he was working on over to another enclosure in the cave and then came back to be with the others to die."

"Really, what killed him?"

"She wasn't sure, but she thought that they had been trapped and were dying of the cold."

"Does she have these visions very often?"

"No, I don't think so, but she has had them before and so has her brother. They claim to have extrasensory perception. You remember Guy thought he saw TemplarKnights and one of them gave him a helmet, which he still has."

"Yes, but I thought that was just something he found in the tunnel when he was trying to escape," said Owain.

In his office the following morning, Owain had a sudden thought. What had happened to the bags of rocks and the old skeletons that were taken from the cave and then placed in the coffins that had been sunk in the bay near The Ormes Victoria Hotel? He wondered. The last he had seen of them was when the coffins were opened in the security room at the West Wales Police Station. To his knowledge these bags of stones were probably still in the security room that had been broken into when relics, coins, and other items of value were stolen. However, the bags of rocks and the skeletons were probably still there. Also as he recalled there had been a skull which Denton removed separately and took away with him when they left the cave when Duvrey first investigated the cave.

He telephoned McDowell who was in the next office. "Listen, Clyde, we have completion work to do on the previous case in North Wales. What happened to the bags of stones and skeleton bones that had been kept in the security room? Would you check on them? They may be of interest to Dr. Holmes and Dr. Grant, who are investigating the cave."

"I will get right on it. As I recall, these items are still there. Did you want them sent to London?"

"No, if the items are still there and the professors are allowed to retrieve them from the police station, that would be best. If they need a court order to remove these items, we will obtain one for them."

"Okay, sir, I will take care of it right now."

Owain got in touch with his wife about his recent thoughts on the case of the items taken from the cave. Joanna was enthusiastic and told Owain that there might be some important items left in the bags. She also mentioned the skull that Bill Denton took.

"Where is Bill Denton right now?"

"In jail awaiting trial," Owain told her.

Final Crises in the Old Cave

Brian and Edward had just received word from Inspector McDowell to come over to the police station in North Wales. They immediately grabbed their coats, and locked up the on-site lab in the trailer near the cave. Brian went over to the cave entrance and made sure the door was secured.

At police headquarters, they had gone down to the security room to check on the items still there after the investigation of the break-in. The station was putting new schedules and new personnel in place. As they entered the room, they located the bags of rocks and the boxes of bones. The coffins also remained there. The persons who had originally occupied the coffins had been placed in new coffins and reburied in the grave yard next to the church in Dewi Sant.

Professor Holmes and Professor Grant entered the police station and were taken down to the security room. First, they checked each bag and the boxes of bones and then compared them to the photos Sgt. McDowell had given them before. Making their way up to their car they loaded the boxes and bags into the back of the vehicle. . . Brian and Edwards returned to the front desk and signed the official papers that gave them the right to take these items with them.

"What a stroke of luck. Thank goodness Owain remembered where they were," Edward said. "We can examine the rocks to find out if there was a reason for Ted Sutter to take them out—or did he just want to give the impression that he had found a vein of gold?"

Brian said that he thought he could locate *the skull* retrieved by Bill Denton if Denton had brought it over to university. The labs had storage areas that Brian could check out. There must be something that attracted Professor Denton to that skull.

"We will be very busy examining all this new evidence. Maybe we should close down the cave and put our efforts into the labs," Edward said. "The data that we have and will have has to be documented. There are so many pieces to the puzzle of the cave's inhabitants."

By the time they had returned to university and their labs with the boxes and heavy bags, they had attracted several of the department's staff, plus students and more of their professor colleagues. Three messages were on their desks. Obviously, curiosity had been raised at the police station and now at the university. No one was sure why the interest in the cave had started again. But everyone was glad to forget about the sad events that had brought about the demise of their friend and colleague Glyn Anderson.

Back in London, Joanna was dying of curiosity about the items that had been forgotten and left in the security room at the police station.

Brian and Edward took off for supper and were surrounded by friends asking question after question concerning their project. Both of them tried to put off their colleagues with technical boring answers in an effort to divert interest and attention away from curiosity about their project. This would only work for a while, though. At some point Brian and Edward were going to have to take a few technicians and specialists into their confidence.

Tired but curious to the point of not being able to sleep, they took out pad and paper to put together a logical program of investigation into all this new material and the possible evidence for the old habitation of the cave.

"We have sectioned off the floor of the cave," Brian started. "But we have not investigated the various side tunnels where Ted found the rock specimens, and then we have the skeleton to be categorized and dated, which includes the skull. We must locate this item; hopefully it is in our storage area, where Denton left it. The rocks have to be examined as well. Thank goodness we have McDowell's photographs." said Brian.

Edward said, "I am worried that this project will need more specialized assistances to guide us. We can't handle this project alone. So, we need to make a list of those who we want to bring in on the project."

The next morning Brian and Edward started their first research and cataloging of what they had brought back to their lab. The rocks had quartz veins in them and some very small flecks of gold, but not enough to warrant a big mining operation. Perhaps the rocks had been enough to encourage investors? For the time being they could be put in storage, so they set them aside. The bones were in Edward's area of study. He looked them over carefully and did some testing but came up with no solid conclusions except that they were male and not more than a few hundred years old. This was not encouraging for their investigation into proving very old inhabitants had been using the cave.

"Still, I need to do more testing on the bones and bring in another expert to confirm my analysis. They do not appear to be from the same person. So we have partial skeletons of more than one male, a missing skull, and not much else to go on."

"You know," added Brian, "the gold jewelry items that were stolen might have been associated with these bones. What happened to those items when they were retrieved from Denton and Older? "

"I imagine that the gold items were sent to the British Museum, and they are in the museum's vaults."

"Could it be that our best opportunity to find some answers is back at the cave?"

"Let's go then, we are wasting more time here. . . .I would like to find the marks on the side of the cave that Ted Sutter made when he gathered up these rocks. We have never taken the time to explore those tunnel s before."

Back at the cave entrance, Brian and Edward found Joanna and Gwyneth looking for them. They claimed to have been hiking nearby, and came over to say hello. Brian smiled and then in the nicest way possible. He tried to encourage them to go back to hiking. The girls left realizing they didn't want help.

Brian and Edward entered the cave again and turned on the generator to give them some light. Then they headed to one of two tunnels that opened off the main cave area. They took large torches and worked their way down the first tunnel. There were markings on the floor and walls of recent activity. The tunnels themselves were large enough to partially stand up in. Further down, they could make out the marks of tools. Then further into the tunnel the air seemed contaminated. Continuing on, both men began to feel dizzy.

"I think we'd better go back and find out what is contaminating the air. It may be a gas that is odorless but very dangerous."

As they turned to go back, Brian bent over to pick up some broken objects on the floor. He noticed in the beam of light from his torch that there were many more pieces lying around; too many for him to carry back. So he had to be satisfied carrying one large piece with him to show Edward after they were safely out of the bad air.

Finally reaching the opening of the large cave chamber, they made their way out into the fresh air. Edward walked over to Brian, who was holding a flat piece of stone.

"Brian, did you carry that object back with you? I am afraid that you over-exerted yourself in that bad air. What have you there? " Edward asked.

Brian had slumped to his knees and put the flat oblong piece on the ground in front of him. Edward got down and was shocked at what he saw. The object was a flat oblong piece of something that resembled a smooth, hard tile, with markings on both sides. The markings were just like the ones they had found on the small pieces from the cave, as well as the pieces that Joanna found in the Bahamas.

Edward helped Brian to his feet and asked, "Should I take you to emergency or will you be all right? Here, take some deep breaths."

"Yes, just give me a few minutes. Put the tile in the car and bring the pieces from the trailer. We will take all of them back to university for security," Brian gasped as he tried to move towards the car. Edward helped him into the car and went back to collect the tile and other pieces. He carefully wrapped them in towels, placed them in a box, and then padlocked the cave.

Joanna and Gwyneth, after being turned away by Brian and Edward from investigating the cave, continued back to their Land Rover, which was parked at a lot for hikers' vehicles.

Gwyneth looked at Joanna with a worried expression on her face.

"What is wrong, Gwyneth?"

"*I sense that something is wrong at the cave.* We must return there and see what it is."

"Gwyneth," said Joanna. "Brian and Edward made it quite clear that we were not to stay. They did not want us to help."

"No, Joanna, something has happened to them."

As Joanna drove the Land Rover up the rutted road to the cave, she saw Edward's car moving towards them very slowly. Joanna stopped the Land Rover and got out. She ran over to their car, which had stopped. Then she called to her friend.

"We need to get them to the hospital, Gwyneth! You drive my vehicle and I will follow you in their car. Brian is unconscious and Edward is almost unconscious."

Soon, both vehicles pulled into the emergency area and attendants came out to help take the two men to an examining room. Joanna went to the desk and filled out the forms for the patients. One of the doctors came out and asked the girls to explain what had happened.

"We went back to their investigation site at the cave. Before we reached the cave, Edward's car was heading towards us very slowly. I jumped out and stopped the car and realized that Brian and Edward needed emergency help."

"You did the right thing and probably saved their lives. They are suffering from gas asphyxiation."

The next day when Joanna returned to the hospital to see her friends, she was told that they had recovered nicely and that she could see them. As Joanna entered their room, Edward spoke. "Hello! And thank you for saving us."

"Gwyneth had another one of her visions of trouble and it involved the two of you at the cave. So we drove over there to check it out. What were you doing that involved breathing in deadly gas?"

"We had been investigating one of the tunnels where Ted Sutter had found his rock samples. We both felt queer and left. On the way, Brian overexerted himself carrying a heavy oblong tile. Where is our car, by the way?"

"We parked your car in the hospital parking lot."

"Great! We have to get out of here and return to our labs at the university."

Joanna helped them check out of the hospital. The doctors wanted to make sure they were well enough to go. Joanna followed them in her car to make sure that they made it back to their flat alright. Upon arriving, Edward asked her to help bring up the objects in the boot. She was glad to assist. She took one look at the large oblong tile and knew right away that this was a large piece of the same type as the smaller ones that she had found. She brought up the smaller pieces but asked for help with the large oblong piece, which looked like a tablet. Edward went back for the large piece. While he was retrieving the object from the boot, one of his students arrived to help. Edward grabbed a robe that he kept in the car and covered the piece with it. The student carried it up to Edward's flat and asked what the object was. Edward just passed it off as a possible runic stone from Nordic times. Joanna realized that it was time to leave; maybe in a few days they would confide in her about the object.

The safety inspector's office was appraised of the gas poisoning of the two men. The Office of Mine Safety determined that the cave should be closed off for any more investigation. However, Chief Inspector Wallon used his contacts to convince them that the professors would take appropriate steps to insure their safety. Gas masks would be used at all times and equipment would be brought in to record the gas levels.

Owain went to see Brian and Edward after he had talked with the Mine Safety people. As Owain explained to Brian and Edward, this was only a *temporary* period during which they could investigate the tunnel and cave. The place had been vandalized at least once. There was always the possibility that more treasure-seekers would try again to find items of value.

"By the way, which tunnel did you say you went into? I have been in one of the tunnels with other officers and we didn't have any problem. Of course we did not go very far away from the cave opening. Then there was the time that Ted Sutter went down one of the tunnels."

Edward said, "We went into the one to the far left from the entrance to the cave."

"I see," said Owain. "We entered the one to the right of that one. Maybe no one else has been down that tunnel that you entered. How far in did you go?"

"Quite a ways, I would say. We saw no markings on the walls and no footprints in the soft dust of the floor. Maybe Ted Sutter never went into the tunnel that we did. That could explain why he didn't have any trouble with gas."

Brian spoke then. "We have to go back into the tunnel again and maybe even further. I found that tablet just as we were turning around to leave. If we are very careful and wear gas masks, plus take frequent readings of the gas meter, we should be alright."

"I would not go down there again and I feel sure that the officials will decide to bulldoze the opening soon. If you want to do any more investigating, I would think twice about it." Owain rose to his feet and left Brian and Edward with deep concern showing on their faces.

Brian said, "We must find a way to do as much as we can right away with as little attention raised as possible. First we have to buy the gear that we need and return to the cave."

"Yes, you are right, except we need a backup person to stay in the cave to make sure that if we do have trouble, they can go for help. Then we need another suit and gear for them. What about Joanna?"

They contacted Joanna about helping them. She was enthusiastic and promised she would not say anything to Owain about their plans. Joanna in turn made arrangements to go stay at Gwyneth's for a few days. It would work out perfectly. He would be unaware of their plans for reentering the cave.

A few days later, Brian, Edward, and Joanna made their way with the suits and gas masks plus measuring equipment and helmet lights and torches, into the cave. They had parked the Land Rover over behind the trailer with their lab setup.

Once in the cave, they set up a place for Joanna to wait while they searched the tunnel again. Each man had a rope around his waist just in case he needed help returning. Joanna would keep track of the rope wheels and she also had her own gauge to check the gas levels in the cave. Brian set the time that they would return. Both men entered the same tunnel to the left that they had entered before.

Once inside the tunnel, they took a reading and agreed that the gas level was low. Going on further and further into the tunnel the gas levels stayed low. Finally their footprints from their previous foray ended. The readings again were low, so they continued on. Then the amount of rope they had allowed themselves gave out.

"I thought you said that you had seen more of those tiles," Edward said.

"They seem to be gone. The tiles should have been about here. Wait a minute—I think I see one just ahead."

With that Brian unbuckled the end of his rope and headed on. Edward called out to him that he didn't think it was a good idea. Then he checked his gas gauge and saw that the level had started to rise. Edward called out to Brian.

"The gas level is rising! We must leave."

Brian stumbled back carrying another tablet. *"Hurry! We must go back!* The gas level is rising."

Both men started the return trek. Brian did not buckle on his rope but Edward told him to walk in front of him. In the meantime, Joanna was nervous; the time for their return had passed. She watched with misgivings the entrance to the tunnel. Outside she could hear men working with machinery. Could they be bulldozing dirt in front of the cave entrance? Was it possible that the work crew did not know that she and the others were in the cave? Waiting as long as she could, she went toward the entrance of the cave to see what was happening. Sure enough, she was right—that was exactly what the work crew was doing. Trees were being put across the entrance and dirt was being shoveled towards her.

She ran out and shouted "Stop! Stop!"

The foreman heard her and stopped the bulldozers with commands in Welsh which she did not understand. He then yelled at her; finally he came over and asked her in plain English to leave.

Joanna explained to him that Brian and Edward were inside. The foreman headed into the cave.

Just then police cars arrived on the scene. Owain jumped out of the lead car.

"Why are here?"– Owain shouted at her. Joanna turned in surprise to see him running toward her.

"Brian and Edward are in the cave, down in the left tunnel, over there," directed Joanna. Owain started for the tunnel opening. Joanna called out to him as she looked at her gauge and realized the gas level was rising. "Don't go down there, the gas level is rising. You need my mask.- Take mine." She quickly unfastened her mask and gave it to him.

It was then that Owain noticed the ropes and started pulling on one. The foreman came over. He asked Owain, "what are you doing?" He told the foreman that down the tunnel each of the men had a rope attached to his waist and we must try to pull on the ropes to get them to come out. There is danger of gas. Then Joanna stepped over and grabbed the other rope and started to vigorously pull on it. This one was Brian's rope. In the tunnel, Brian watched his rope slither past him as Edward and he were making their way back. Edward noticed the rope move past him also. Then he felt a strong tug on his rope.

Unnoticed by Joanna and Owain the foreman slowly backed up and headed towards the entrance, then ran out of the cave. As soon as he was out of their sight, the foreman made a dash for his workmen.

Back in the tunnel, Edward said, "Joanna must be trying to contact us. Hurry, Brian, I will take the tablet now." Both men picked up their pace and would soon see the light from the tunnel opening.

Observing Brian's untied rope emerging into the cave, Joanna gave a groan. Owain exclaimed, "Joanna you told me they had ropes tied around their waists."

"They do," answered Joanna, "and the one that I am holding is taut, – so it must be around one of their waists. They should be close. Wait! I see them."

Both Brian and Edward cleared the tunnel entrance and came into the cave. One was carrying a tablet and the other one did not have his rope attached.

"Hurry! The gas level has started to rise again." Joanna, who was the only one without a gas mask, was coughing. Owain grabbed Joanna and ran for the entrance, followed by Edward with the tablet and Brian close on his heels. As they cleared the cave entrance and headed for the Land Rover they saw that the earth-moving machines moving fast up the road. Thinking that there would be an explosion, the police cars moved back to let them through.

Chief Inspector Owain Wallon made his way over to the foreman and asked him in Welsh for his work-order papers. Waving, the foreman backed away and jumped on to one of the large bulldozers that were heading down the road. Owain shouted to the policemen to block their way. As soon as the workmen and the foreman realized that they were trapped, they ran off into the woods with the police in hot pursuit. The officers returned soon to say that they had caught the workers who were running away. They were being taken to headquarters and the superintendent would await his orders.

Owain with concern in his voice called over to Joanna, Brian and Edward. "What are you doing here? All of you know the cave is dangerous with methane gas in the air." He never thought they did not understand the dangers in the cave and would attempt to go in the cave again.

Joanna who was surprised to encounter Owain at the cave with his police team, called back to Owain "What are *you* doing here? I thought you were out of the area on a confidential drug case somewhere else."

"I am investigating the cave as a storage area that a drug dealer uses. Owain told her. "We recently discovered that the drug dealers were using the cave as a hideout."

Brian took the tablet from Edward and put it carefully in the back of the Land Rover out of sight. Joanna joined them. Owain left in his police car and returned to police headquarters. He intended to report the dealer's activities in the cave.

Back at The Ormes Victoria Hotel, Joanna, Brian, and Edward sat at the bar and tried to piece together what had happened in such a short time. Tom joined the group and listened to the discussion in sheer amazement. "Where is Owain? I guess we interfered in his roundup of some drug dealers." Brian said.

Edward said, "I guess they decided to block off the entrance to the cave despite what Owain had told us. The officials of the Mine Safety Board moved fast to cut off the entrance."

"Those crazy workmen nearly buried us alive in that cave," Brian said furiously.

Gwyneth joined them. She suggested that maybe that was what happened to the little girl and her family. They were trapped in the cave where they took shelter from the cold. A new Ice Age was taking over the land where they had lived for centuries. They tried to leave some of their knowledge behind and the knowledge was on the tablets; but we don't know what the tablets tell us." Gwyneth was referring to the vision that she had had while in the cave a few days ago.

Edward and Brian were trying to accept the fact that their project was lost. The cave was declared dangerous and closed off to any further research. When they had tried to investigate the cave after Glyn Anderson's death, the gas levels caused them to collapse and go to emergency. After the next time, they tried to investigate the tunnel for more tiles, the gas was there again. This time they had gas masks on as a precaution. The park authorities where now determined to stop anyone from entering the cave for their own safety.

"That is true," commented Brian. "Even if we cannot reenter the cave we have extracted enough material, plus the tablets, to keep our research going for some time." Everyone agreed and they were glad that they all got out safely.

Joanna left her friends still conversing in the lounge. She was depressed. Owain was upset with her. She felt unhappy with him. Opening the door to her room, she found Owain sitting on the edge of the bed waiting for her.

"Come on in. I have something to tell you; and I hope that it will make both of us feel better. I am taking a leave of absence from Scotland Yard. Sir Gordon agrees. Good old Hadley has called friends of his in Bangor; and I will be offered a visiting professorship in the criminology department. If you like we can leave the flat in London and rent a nice house near university. How does that sound to you?" Owain looked at her with such an expression of love in his eyes and continued. "My work is pitting us against each other; and I don't want that to happen. This opportunity at university for a year will give us a time to be together."

"Oh, yes, Owain I think that it would be just wonderful." Joanna pushed away a tear in her eye.

E p i l o g u e :

The goldmine and the remaining treasures had been saved from the plans of Shedweld and his team of robbers. The old cave which had survived for centuries continued to retain the old mysteries for future explorations.

In the end, Chief Inspector Owain Wallon brought the three murder cases to a satisfactory conclusion. Shedweld's business operations were fully uncovered and the money was traced to Singapore. However, the bond and gold had been transferred to an underworld tai-pan.

Owain's aunt and uncle divulged the story of his father. Joanna and Owain had fallen madly in love during her stressful period of criminal accusations made out against her. They married in true British style.

Made in the USA
Coppell, TX
19 May 2023

17028653R00105